Pond People

Cathy Cade

Also by Cathy Cade

A Year Before Christmas
Witch Way and other ambiguous stories
The Godmother

Cover by John Spiers
https://jrspierswriter.com

For my children and their children.

Pond People

Contents

Acknowledgements

Thanks are due to the Whittlesey Wordsmiths for their continuing encouragement.

Especial thanks go to John Spiers for his gorgeous cover illustration.

Follow John's blog at https://mylifewithgracie.com//

1 Flash Lightning

A tiny black swimmer glided below the surface as the morning sun warmed the water. Its shade travelled the pond floor and passed over a dozing bronze sleeper basking in filtered sunlight, his eyes glazed and his feet twitching. Above him, at the edge of the pond, goldfish grazed.

Slender arms broke away from the swimmer's sides and fins became hands to sweep the water and steady her descent. Her tail parted to become legs, touching down on flat, triangular feet which, moments ago, had served as tail fins.

The sleeper on the pond floor shivered as a shadow blocked his sunlight. Fish dived and scattered.

A watcher concealed in the watermint glanced up through the surface ripples. A black cat rose from its crouch and padded around the pond to the warm brick paving at the end.

At the bottom of the pond, eyes moved in the weathered bronze face.

'Molly, lass. How are things at the deeps?'

'Things are stirring.' She ran webbed fingers through hair that clung to her shoulders like blanketweed. 'The fish are on the move now the weather's warmer.'

A watcher in the watermint strained to catch the conversation.

'Your feet were twitching, Grandad. Were you dreaming?'

'Aye, lass. I was back in the river, riding a rain surge with the sticklebacks and dodging the stones. Don't suppose I could do that now without getting battered.'

His gills laboured as he eyed the waterfall across the pond. The old mirling was missing a scale or two. He took a blade from his belt of plaited blanketweed to carve a sliver from the reed behind him.

The watcher coveted both belt and blade. Had his own people made things like this? The pond mirlings he'd met since he arrived had been tame and easy to impress, but this old mirling was raised in wilder waters.

Molly had sneaked away early from the deep end before her parents filled her day with spawn-watching and her head with instructions. She'd rather fill both with Grandad's memories of his river.

Grandad wintered with the other mirlings in deeper water, but when the sun grew strong enough to warm the shallows, he would move here to be close to the waterfall.

No fish or mirling rode the pond's waterfall. It cascaded from the filter outlet, high above the deeps, and its channel formed a wall around half the pond. Birds came to drink and splash in the water that sparkled over its stones.

It emptied into the shallows, where people from the house came to scatter fish food, and where a goldfish now grazed under the watchful eye of the cat.

Molly saw the cat tense at the same time as Grandad shouted.

But fish aren't frightened of mirlings. This one carried on nibbling its way towards the cat.

Molly launched.

A paw descended, dark as death. She found herself hurtling into a swipe that would scoop both fish and mirling out of the water.

Something streaked past Molly, washing her aside and propelling the goldfish into the cover of reeds. The cat's paw rose empty through the water.

The bright blur swooped into a somersault before slowing to become an orange-and-black mirling. He landed with a flourish in front of Grandad and two watching youngsters, while Molly fought to re-establish which way was up.

'Hi, kids. The name's Flash. They call me Flash Lightning.'

His iridescent orange glistened in the watery sunlight. A contrasting black streak fell rakishly across the left side of his spiky hair, across one eye and down the side of a muscular body. Molly had to admit he was an impressive looking mirling.

And no one was more impressed than Flash.

Drawing himself up to his full two centimetres, Flash noted with satisfaction that he was taller than his audience, although he thought the old mir might have matched him in his youth, before his bronze back stooped.

'Well done, lad! That were fast.'

'I like to keep fit.'

A scrawny yellow youngster groaned quietly.

It was a groan, not a thoughtwave, but Flash's hearing was excellent, and the ear-slits in front of his gills caught the sound. He'd seen this undersized runt at the pump, where fit mirlings exercised by swimming against its pull. This strawhead had disrupted their training with his irritating pranks.

A new voice crept into his head. 'Aren't you the m-mirling who came with the fish from the pet shop?'

The pale mirling who'd asked was a head shorter than the others, skinny as a water-reed and as plain, but her cream-coloured eyes glowed with admiration around their inky pupils. He rewarded her with a smile.

'You noticed me then.'

Her flat, white face flushed pink.

'Flo notices more than people realise.'

The speaker was the black swimmer he had swept aside in his dash to the goldfish. Her scales seemed to absorb light instead of reflecting it. His proud colours suddenly felt garish.

He turned to the rosy white one. 'Then you must be Flo.'

She flushed deeper as the old mirling nodded. 'Yep, that's Flo, and this here is Molly.' He rested his hand on the dark one's shoulder. 'Call me Grandad, everyone does. The clown over there is Flo's brother, Eddy.'

The strawhead had drifted away to make faces at the cat, which settled to wait for another fish.

Flo frowned. 'There m-must be something we can do about that cat.'

Flash turned to the old mir. 'You can't have always been called Grandad.'

'No. Me sister were named Penny, for a coin that lay in the river, and I were Tuppence.' He shook his head. 'It in't a name to grow old with.'

'So, how did you come to the pond?'

2   Eddy and Flo

'I'm river mir, born and bred.' Grandad squared his shoulders. 'Had a mate and a son when I were netted with some sticklebacks by children who lived in the house back then. I recall their Pa weren't best pleased when they emptied their bucket into the pond.'

'Are there others here from the river?' Flash asked.

'No. We were all born here,' Molly answered. 'Our great-grandparents came with the fish that stocked the pond.'

'Were your family in the pet shop t-too?'

He shook his head.

'Just me.'

He'd been out swimming with the fish when men came to trawl their pond and he was caught up with the shoal. As a vivid orange mirling with nowhere to hide in the featureless pet shop tanks, he'd learned to swim in the shadows of the fish and keep his dark side towards the outside world.

'I had to look after myself. If staff spotted mirlings in a tank, they'd think they were parasites and empty the tank to disinfect it.' He had their full attention. 'Any mir too slow to cling to a fish would be left in the empty tank.'

Flo's eyes widened. 'W-what happened to them?'

'I never saw one again to ask.'

He leaned against a water-iris. 'When the tank was emptied, they'd be washed down a drain to be eaten by a rat or poisoned by sewage. Or they could cling to the empty tank and dehydrate.'

Dehydration was a slow death. Their horror infused the surrounding water, diluting his own recurrent nightmare.

Something dropped from above, knocking Flo into Grandad, who staggered.

'Eddy!' shouted Molly and Flo in unison. Eddy grinned.

'Sorry.' Flo flushed pink. 'He thinks he's funny. Are you alright, Grandad?'

'Don't worry, lass. Takes more than a shove to upset an old river-rat.'

Flash was about to continue his interrupted account, but Molly cut in. 'Tell Flash about your river, Grandad.'

The old mir's eyes misted. 'Ah, the river… it went on forever. The water were always fresh.' Around them, the water held memories of bluebell and evening primrose.

'The plants was thick for hiding in. They grew on the bottom too.' All eyes went to the pond's black liner. 'Mind you, there were plenty to hide from. We was food to the bigger fish.'

Eddy frowned. 'But the pond fish don't eat us.'

'That's because they kn-now us.'

'Summat like that,' agreed Grandad. 'Goldfish in't wild like river fish. They's domesticated, like dogs and cats. And they gets fed reg'lar.'

'But they still eat the small fry.' Eddy frowned. 'And that's their own family.'

This was news to Flash. In his home pond, new-laid spawn and hatched fry were separated from adult fish. He kept quiet and listened.

'I don't think fish realise the fry are their own hatchlings.' Grandad watched a goldfish swim past. 'Fish in't very clever. If it moves, they catch it – no time to decide if it's a baby or a bug.'

'Maybe mirlings don't taste good,' suggested Molly.

'They don't know that till they've tried us,' Flo pointed out.

Grandad shrugged. 'The river fish never minded our taste. No more did the ducks, or the heron watching from the shallows, or the land creatures that swam after us. At least the cat don't do that. Cats don't like water.'

Flash hadn't known that either. He wondered what else the old codger knew that might come in useful.

These pond mirlings were soft, but he couldn't afford to look stupid. Here in the pond he could safely glory in his striking colours, but he would be wise to keep his darker side hidden.

Molly loved hearing about Grandad's river, but she wouldn't want to live there. Here, they shared the pond with nothing more threatening than mayflies, water boatmen and goldfish. And other mirlings. Grandad said everyone looked after each other when there were real threats to cope with, but she couldn't believe he really missed being at the mercy of water voles. And herons, whatever they were. She pictured a heron as a different kind of cat.

'There must be something we can do about that cat.'

Flash's brow creased. 'It doesn't hunt mirlings though, does it? It doesn't come in the pond?'

Flash's sprint had been all for show – she'd suspected as much. He didn't care about saving the goldfish. She tried to explain in a way he would understand.

'They're *our* fish the cat's taking. We've watched them grow.'

Not that she felt any fondness for them when it was her turn to shoo them away from water plants heavy with their spawn.

'We protect the spawn and hatchlings so at least some of them survive. We don't do all that so the neighbour's cat can eat them instead.'

She dismissed a shadow of guilt. It was her brother's turn. Time he did his share of herding small fry, instead of spending his days kicking a pellet around the pond floor with his pals.

'And w-when you've trained one,' Flo added, 'and it's learned to trust you, it's heart-breaking to find it's gone from the pond.'

'You train them?' Flash looked interested now.

Grandad explained. 'The gentle ones gets taught to carry mirlings on their backs, so us oldies can ride without having to cling on like fish lice.'

Eddy's eyes glowed. 'Some are untrainable–'

'Only because they're m-more sensitive.'

'–and they try to throw you off. We take bets on who can stay up longest.' He weaved and ducked to illustrate the perils of rough riding.

Flo ignored him.

'We could take turns to w-watch for the cat.' She reddened when everyone looked at her. 'Draw up a rota…' her words drifted away.

Molly usually listened to Flo. She came up with some good ideas. This wasn't one of them.

'Sorry girls.' Flash saluted. 'You'll have to count me out. Too busy.'

'Busy posing at the pump.' Eddy muttered from a safe distance.

'Cat's gone,' announced Grandad. 'Must be feeding time.'

The head of a tan and white terrier appeared over the edge of the pond. Mojo, the dog from the house, didn't approve of cats in his garden. His tongue lapped the water, sending out ripples to meet those from the waterfall.

Behind the dog a man tapered towards the sky. Pellets of fish food plopped into the water. Their fishy smell drifted to Molly's nostrils.

Fish came from every direction. Within seconds the pellets were almost gone, and the feeding frenzy began to quieten.

Out among the feeders, Eddy hovered over a young fish. He made contact in front of its dorsal fin, and it shook to throw him off. He whooped with delight as it bucked and plunged towards the deeps.

Molly watched until they were out of sight in the churning water. She turned to see Flash watching too before he looked away.

'What an idiot!' He waved. 'See you later, girls. Nice to meet you, Grandad. Good luck with that cat.' He took off with a flick of his body.

Flo stood behind her. 'Give him a chance, M-molly. He's got n-nobody.'

'He doesn't need anybody. I'm sure he can do everything he wants to all by himself.'

'He may have saved your l-life.'

Molly resisted that thought.

It was he who'd decided she needed rescuing. She owed him nothing. Her throat tightened again at the memory of her fear, quickly displaced by the indignity of being pushed aside, like… like something in the way.

'Eddy doesn't like him either.' Flo sighed. 'I'd hoped he might make friends with the n-newcomer and stop following that crowd that see him as their court jester.'

'That'll never happen.' Molly snorted. 'They're too different. Your Eddy takes nothing seriously, and Flash takes himself very seriously indeed.'

3 Anything You Can Do

The pump lay at the bottom of the deep end, drawing in tired water that had travelled the pond. Its pull was strong enough to drive water to the filter at the top of the waterfall where it would begin its journey again.

Around the pump, keep-fit enthusiasts worked out by swimming against its drag, and any swooping fish or thrown rider would disrupt their training.

Flash watched the rough riders while he was working out. An untrained dodger-fish would instinctively head for deep water when a mirling landed on its back, so riders soon found themselves above the swimmers at the pump. Or among them.

If these idiots could ride the leaping fish, how hard could it be?

Like everyone else, he shouted at the riders, but now he noted which fish they rode. Once he was sure he would recognise them again, he left the swimmers at the pump and headed for the shallows.

He wanted to hear more about life in the river.

Grandad sat with Flo, trimming a young reed with the blade that Flash could now see was a sharpened snail shell.

Flo looked up through the ripples as drops of rain dappled the pond's surface. Flo looked up through the ripples as drops of rain dappled the pond's surface.

'C-cat's gone.'

Flash touched down beside Grandad, pleased that the snooty black one wasn't with them. Pasty little Flo was friendlier, and Grandad seemed pleased to see him.

'Flash! You're a sportsman. How are you at spitting?'

'Spitting?'

'Have you never taken part in a spitting contest, lad? Come on, see if you can beat me.'

Flash and Flo followed him up to the surface. Grandad straddled a lily stem and filled his gills; heads had to be out of water to spit. He filled his mouth and raised his head to spit water at a nearby lily flower. After several hits, he rested on a stem beneath the water.

The rain had stopped by the time Flash perfected his aim, but he wasn't going to let an old codger beat him – not even an old river codger. It was a point of honour to be best at whatever he tried.

He'd forgotten about Flo, who waited until he had finished before taking aim. It was a shock when she hit her target first time.

'I've been practising with Eddy,' she admitted, 'but I could never spit as far as you can.'

'Never say never, lass.' Grandad produced the hollow reed he'd brought with him. 'Here, try this. You blows the water through.'

Flo was soon targeting leaves outside the pond, and Flash was impatient to try it. Before they swam down, Grandad took the reed for some trial shots of his own.

Flash watched closely, looking for tips. Might this reed shoot underwater? Solid missiles perhaps?

The stem would eventually weaken with use. He would need a blade if he were to make his own reed shooters.

Molly had been delayed by her father lecturing on the responsibilities that came with living in leafy luxury, on a plant where goldfish went to spawn.

His words echoed around her head like an old song. It was time she started pulling her weight. Perhaps she'd prefer a life in the mud, or sleeping rough in a fold of the pond liner?

She could recall nobody from school she would want to live with, which eliminated half the eligible pond life. How did you choose a life partner anyway? What if, later on, you got to know someone you liked better?

On the other hand, she didn't want to spend her life herding hatchlings or teaching tiddlers in one of the pond's summer schools. She wasn't clever with her hands, like Flo.

Grandad had taught them to plait blanketweed last summer but, while Flo's cords were fine enough to make armlets and necklaces, hers were too lumpy to barter, and she had lost interest.

When she arrived in the shallows, there was no sign of Grandad. She was about to swim home again when that swaggering newcomer zoomed out of the waterlilies.

Flo and Grandad drifted down after him. 'What've you been up to, Grandad?'

'Reed shooting. Come with me.'

He handed her the reed they'd been using and led the way to his den, where he pulled out another length of reed, slightly wider than the first.

'I'm trimming up different lengths and widths, to find out which shoot farthest.'

Flo took the new reed and put it to her lips. 'This one feels too wide in my m-mouth.'

Molly thought it would suit a bigmouth like Flash.

To her surprise, the bigmouth was enthusiastic. 'You could appoint a champion.' He grinned. 'Then other mirlings can challenge him for the title.'

'Or her.' Molly turned to Flo. No cat today?'

'N-not since the rain.'

'How about you, Molly?' asked Grandad. 'Like to try reed shooting?'

'Maybe.'

She knew it wasn't for her, and she saw no practical use for it, but Grandad seemed pleased with himself. 'If enough mirlings was interested, we could get teams together for a tournament.'

Flash nodded. 'You'd need prizes.'

'We'd have to stand people n-near the targets to judge the best hits.' Flo looked doubtful. 'M-mightn't that be dangerous?'

Grandad looked uncertain now. 'Sounds like it'd take some organising.'

'I don't mind helping you organise it,' Molly offered, not wanting to be left out.

'How do you feel about organising a team, then?' asked Grandad.

'Oh, I'd be no good at shooting.'

'How can you tell, lass, if you haven't tried?'

'How about Eddy? Flo tells me he's good at target-spitting.'

A bubble of laughter escaped Flash's mouth. He asked Flo to pass him the wider reed and swam up with it.

Grandad's eyes met Flo's.

When Flash was out of range, he turned to Molly.

'Can you picture Eddy as a team leader? Recruiting members, organising practice sessions, deciding strategy?'

Flo's head was shaking. Molly saw their point. 'But I've never led a team before.'

'Good time ter find out if you can.'

'Why would anyone listen to me, who can't even shoot?'

'Why not?' Grandad shrugged. 'You can manage a team without being a player. There's nowt to stop you appointing Eddy as team coach.'

Flo was nodding. 'And you can always ask if there's something you're not sure about.'

Flash swam down from the surface as Grandad gestured to an imaginary group. 'You can ask your team. They'll like to be consulted. You know how teams work.'

Molly liked being part of a team. Teams were about sharing work. Stealthy herders could circle the hatchlings while the fastest swimmers chased stragglers.

But leading a team… that was scary.

'I'll be a team leader,' announced Flash. 'My team will be Flash's Lightning Strikers. How many to a team?'

'Let's find out if anyone wants to join first.'

'So you'll do it, M-molly?'

Three pairs of eyes were on her. Flash didn't try to hide the amusement in his. How dare he laugh at her?

She wouldn't let *him* put her off. 'I'll see.'

'That's settled then.' Grandad rubbed his hands together. 'How about you, Flo? Going to join Molly's team?'

'Oh no.' Flo shook her head so hard her hair drifted out in a creamy cloud. 'I'd lose my n-nerve at the last minute and let everyone down.'

'Right-ho – you can be Chief Judge.' Flo shrank back. 'Find yourself a couple of assistants and decide how you'll score the hits so there's no argument later.'

He put a finger under her chin and gently closed her mouth. 'I'll help. Now clear off, all of you, and recruit. I needs me afternoon nap.'

4   Tournament Day

Flash recruited his team from the mirlings who trained at the pump. He wanted marksmen who were fit, competitive, and up for a challenge.

He heard that Molly was taking on anyone who wanted to join.

He'd always been able to look after himself and wouldn't rely on others for his success now, but this was an opportunity to gather followers.

After each Lightning Strikers' training session, Flash carried on practising. He had to be the best. That's what leaders were.

During training sessions, he criticised poor performances. A few shooters became discouraged and left. Good riddance if they couldn't improve.

Some of these joined Molly's team.

He called them 'Molly's Misfits' and the name stuck. Apparently, Eddy was coaching them.

The Strikers reckoned Eddy would be his strongest rival, but nobody had seen Molly shoot yet. He didn't trust her. Was she keeping herself undercover as the Misfits' secret weapon?

He couldn't allow Molly to beat him.

Grandad was sharpening a shard of snail shell when Molly walked into his hollow.

'Molly lass, will this do for a trophy, d'you think?' He picked up a solid horn-shape made of bone, or something similar. It had a hole bored through it.

She admired its smooth surface. 'We'll have three teams next year. Eddy's beginners are as good as the others now.'

'Why not this year?' asked Grandad.

'And lose my best shooter? What's that shell for?'

'I'm sharpening a new blade for trimming reed shoots. It's the prize for the most accurate shot. And look at this.' From the flat-topped stone that formed a workbench, he selected a hollow chunk of mature reed. 'I'm carving a victor's crown for whoever shoots the farthest.'

Flo arrived. As they greeted each other a fish darted past. It dived steeply, and a mirling tumbled off. Arms and legs thrashed in a bright orange blur which twisted to land on its feet.

'Look who's taken up rough riding.' Molly folded her arms. 'Now, why am I not surprised?'

With its burden shed, the fish slowed to settle among the lily stems. They watched Flash swim in a circle to approach it from behind and hover, ready to drop into riding position.

Flo shook her head. 'He's landing too fast. Eddy could give him some tips.'

Grandad was behind her. 'He'll want to do it by hisself. I reckon he's practising here 'cos he's checked that Eddy's at the deeps and won't see him fall off.'

'It's a shame.' Flo's thought hung between them.

Grandad looked at her. 'What is?'

'It's a shame Flash won't ask for help. It would do w-wonders for his confidence.'

Molly sniffed. 'I don't think so. He's arrogant enough already.'

'She don't mean Flash.'

Flo explained. 'Eddy was always smaller than the other tiddlers, but the bullies would leave him alone when he m-made them laugh. He started rough riding because they laughed when he fell off at all. Then he got to choose when he fell off and whether he fell off. Rough riding's the only thing he's good at.'

'He's good at reed shooting.'

Flo stared at Molly. 'Is he? He practises a lot.'

'It's paid off. He's good at training others too. They listen to him because he knows what he's talking about, and because they listen, he doesn't clown around.'

Grandad was watching the rough riding. 'Looks like Flash's practice is paying off too.'

They watched the fish hurtle towards the deeps, darting and diving in vain, trying to shake off its rider.

On the morning of the tournament, the sky rippled blue above the pond. The water was already warming as Flash arrived on the back of a goldfish. This one had decided it was easier to ignore its hitchhiker than to throw him and, in spite of its pauses to graze, they arrived earlier than expected.

As competitors began to drift into the shallows, Flash was twitchy and impatient to compete.

Grandad brought out new reeds and started arranging them by width and length.

Flo called her judges together for last-minute instructions.

Fish grazed above them.

He recognised one he'd ridden yesterday. He knew how this one moved, which way it would jump, when it would dive…. After this morning's easy ride, he reckoned he could out-think any dumb fish.

Molly arrived with Eddy looking relaxed and confident.

There was still time to dent that confidence before the tournament started. He'd show them he could do anything Eddy could and do it better.

He hardly disturbed the water as he glided over the fish, sinking slowly, gently, ready for the first dive when the fish felt—

His world lurched.

The goldfish rose through the water, taking him with it. They parted in the air and, for a moment, he flew.

He slammed into the ground, the impact forcing water from his mouth and out of his gills. The flapping fish threatened to crush him until the cat's paw swiped, and the fish flew again. The cat pounced after its new toy, eyes fixed on the flailing goldfish.

For a terrifying moment, Flash couldn't make his arms or legs move.

He heard the waterfall, but he was too far away to see it. He pushed aside blades of grass. His gills burned and he struggled to stand. Moving was hard work out of water.

Once out of the grass, his feet hurt on the hot paving, but now he saw water tumbling down the waterfall and spilling over its edge. Starved of oxygen and drying out, he dropped to his knees and crawled across the burning brick. Nearly there – he glanced over his shoulder.

The cat stood watching from the grass.

He tried to crawl faster, but his arms and legs wouldn't move faster, and the edge wasn't coming closer. With his heartbeat thudding in his ears, his eyes sought the waterfall, willing it nearer.

A blow sent him sideways, rolling over and over until he was back in the grass. He curled over his knees with no strength left to crawl.

The strange insect fascinated the cat.

5   The Winning Shot

Team members greeted each other under the reeds and told each other how nervous they were. Supporters who had arrived early to get a good spot for viewing were becoming restless.

Molly checked off the last of her team to arrive and sent them to join Eddy and the others. Spectators were still arriving. As she took her team list to Flo, she recognised a group of Flash's supporters from last week's friendly match. That plump silver one had complained about her view from the spectator zone.

She was pouting again today. 'Come on, Walter – there's a space over there. Oh, triffic! Someone's beaten us to it.' Tendrils of silver hair trailed across her petulant frown as she glanced behind them. 'Can't she swim any faster?'

Her friend, a pale orange youngster, ran his hand through the pale tufts of hair sticking up on his head.

'It's not my fault, Sylv. It was either looking after Amber, or guarding tadpoles, and then I couldn't have come at all.'

'Why is it always you who has to look after Amber?'

Her shrill protest carried to Molly, but Walter gave no sign that he'd heard. He was watching a frail, half-grown honey-coloured mirling as she swam unevenly towards them.

'Come on, Amber!'

'Coming, Wally.'

'His name's Walter.' Sylva turned away.

Walter scanned the assembled teams. 'Have you spotted Flash yet?'

Molly followed his gaze to where the Strikers were gathering.

The water surged, blurring her vision, and fish darted for cover. A black streak whisked out of sight above the surface ripples.

'Was that the cat? Did anyone see? Did it get a fish?'

The shallows fell silent.

'I think it did,' someone answered. 'I was looking the other way.'

'Spit!' Flo was ashen. 'We forgot to look out for the c-cat.'

A newly arrived Striker touched down, 'Is Flash around?'

'He was here a minute ago,' a teammate answered.

'He swam up to the surface,' another offered. 'Probably gone to check out the targets.'

All eyes rose towards the rim of the pond.

'I thought he was heading for a fish.'

The cat reappeared, pawing playfully at something on the ground.

'Oh, no!' Flo's hand covered her mouth.

Molly launched, issuing instructions as she swam.

'All shooters to the surface. Anyone with a reed, drench that cat!'

Who was she to give orders? as if expecting everyone to jump.

And they did.

'Shoot as hard as you can and as fast as you can. Aim anywhere. Just hit it!'

Grandad handed reeds to anyone who thought they could help. From surface leaves of lilies and reeds and watermint, mirlings aimed with varying degrees of success, dipping to reload between shots. Someone offered her their reed shooter, but she shook her head and watched from just below the surface.

The cat shook itself.

The shooters' aim improved.

The cat turned its head towards the source of the barrage and Eddy scored a direct hit, straight in its eye.

It shook its head and ran – away from this needle-sharp rain that whipped sideways.

Shooting slowed… and stopped.

As the water settled, Molly's view cleared.

Drops trickled off the brick edge, back into the pond.

A shooter dived from her lily stem, followed by another, and then more. Others stayed watching. A clump of dust blew to the edge of the pond and lodged there.

There was no wind.

Molly tried raising her head out of water, but her eyes stung in the dry air and she had to retreat. They still stung in the water. As the surface settled again, she located the grubby clump again. On a neighbouring lily, Grandad dipped his head to take a breath.

The clump gave a heave and rolled into the pond.

It dropped, dust drifting away as it bumped over blanketweed to lay motionless at the bottom. Orange patches now showed through the grime.

She dived.

Flo and Eddy were there before her. Grandad floated down to join them.

Flash's mouth was open and fixed.

Flo knelt over the body, brushing dust out of its gills. She looked up.

'They're m-moving.' Her words barely reached them. 'He's breathing.'

Hardly, thought Molly. That flutter could have been the water's movement.

She looked away.

Eddy was nearly as pale as Flo, his fixed stare as lifeless as Flash's. Grandad squeezed Flo's shoulder.

Her own throat was tight.

A gulp shook the body. Flash winced as his gills opened. His mouth closed, and his eyes moved for the first time.

They found hers.

'Must do something 'bout cat.'

Her hands and toes uncurled as relief washed through her.

Flash's eyes glazed again as 'I owe you,' travelled through the water between them.

'Not me. It was Eddy who hit the cat's-eye.' She knew because she'd heard Grandad congratulate him. 'I don't shoot. I'm air-blind. My eyes don't work out of water.'

Flash's eyes widened and fixed; she thought he'd passed out again. Then he started laughing, which made him cough. His eyes found Eddy, and he managed a nod.

'Thanks mate.' He coughed again. 'That has to be the prizewinning shot.'

A smile broke like sunshine across Eddy's face, lighting his straw-coloured eyes.

'Give you a re-match?'

Flash seemed to consider but may have been gathering energy to reply.

'Only if I get to choose targets next time.'

6 Goldie

Flash insisted he would be well enough to compete next day.

Molly was unconvinced but said nothing. Flo protested and was overruled. The tournament was rescheduled for the following day.

Eddy won the sharpshooting prize; it was a popular win. Molly could sense Flash was doing his best to hide his disappointment. He unwound after he won the long-distance shoot and was cheered by both sides. Prizegiving would take place at the deeps the following afternoon.

When Molly joined Flo and Grandad in the morning, they were packing the prizes into a bag of woven blanketweed.

'I've come to help – any excuse to get away from watching fry hatch. Trying to herd those little wrigglers is like trying to catch a sneeze in a spider-web.'

Few would survive in spite of their efforts.

Flash and Eddy lurched past on a young carrot-coloured goldfish that Flash struggled to steer. When the fish decided to stop and graze on pondweed, its riders gave up and swam over.

'That reminds me.' Flo raised a hand. 'I've organised a ride for us this afternoon, Grandad. She's a sturdy old fish. There'll be room for a couple more if anyone wants a lift.'

'I'll ride with you,' offered Molly.

'Not for us, thanks.' Eddy pointed to their former mount. 'We're breaking in this dodger for riding.'

He turned to check that the fish was still feeding. 'He's given up trying to throw me, so we're riding him tandem to get him used to carrying more weight.'

Distant shouts came from the world above, bursting into the garden from the house.

One of the children appeared at the edge of the pond, fumbling with something in his hand. His sister ran up, screaming at him between sobs.

Their father's voice came from the house and thundered across the garden.

'Joel, don't!'

'But Dad, she can't keep it in a bag.'

'Goldie's mine.' the girl sobbed. 'I won him. He's mine!'

Seen from the bottom of the pond, the girl's dark head and fists contrasted with the boy's white t-shirt as she his chest. He held something high, out of her reach.

The shadow of their bigger brother fell across them. 'Don't b-be mean, Joel. Give it b-back to her.'

'Now!' their father barked, sounding nearer.

'Aw, man.' The boy flung the object into the pond and ran off.

On the surface a bubble floated, enclosed in a clear bag. A small female goldfish flicked back and forth inside its own watery world. Then a net dipped, and it was gone.

'Here you are, love. But what are you going to do with it? Joel's right, you know. You can't keep it in a bag.'

'I don't want Goldie to go in the pond. I can't talk to him in the pond.'

Her voice changed direction. 'I want him indoors, Mummy, where I can see him.'

A woman spoke, unseen by the mirlings. 'Oh, Bethany… I suppose it could go in that terrarium the Wilsons gave us last Christmas. I don't think I threw it away when the plants died.'

'What's a tare'um, Mummy?'

'It's a glass bowl to grow plants in. I'll see if I can find it.'

The child ran with her prize into the house and her mother groaned. 'Just what I need – a fish tank to clean out.'

'Is a terrarium like a fish tank then?' asked her eldest son.

'No, but you can't keep fish in a bowl for long.' She turned towards the house. 'Let's hope she gets fed up with it in a couple of days and it can go in the pond.' Her voice became fainter. 'We'll tell her it's lonely.'

Bewilderment tinged the water, and Molly realised Flash didn't understand the humans. She had grown up listening to them in the garden, but people in a pet shop probably didn't say much more than, 'That orange goldfish, please,' or 'A tub of fish food.'

Some of the bewilderment was Flo's.

'Did she say she *won* that fish?'

Grandad explained.

'Travelling fairs used to give away goldfish as prizes, but I thought they'd stopped. Nobody's brought one home for years.'

'What's going to happen to that poor fish now they've taken it inside?'

Flo's eyes were large in her pale face, but nobody could answer her.

Molly sat behind Flo and Grandad on the bigger fish, ready to set off for the prizegiving in the deeps.

She turned to watch Eddy settle behind Flash on the smaller fish. Behind them, at the pond's edge, a bucket dipped below the surface. Water flowed over its rim and the bucket rose.

She followed its dark mass from the water to the pond edge, where a blurry human knelt watching the fish. Like the cat did.

Sometimes water was taken like this when the pond became cloudy or blanketweed threatened to block the pump. With luck, Molly's group would be gone from the shallows before the water was returned with something unpleasant added. Such treatments were diluted by the time they reached the deeps.

They were ready to leave. Molly turned back, sensing the suppressed energy from the younger fish as Flash persuaded it to swim beside the stately old glider.

The water rocked, and suddenly a net rose beneath them.

The fish thrashed, throwing Molly into the netting which now surrounded them all. She tried to avoid the flailing fish as they were dragged from the water.

A giant hand tipped the net inside out, and she dropped into water again, this time surrounded by black walls. She drifted to the bottom of the bucket while the fish shook out their tails and circled above with Flash darting between them. The sky had shrunk to a circle.

Other mirlings cowered around the base of the bucket. There was Eddy… and two – no, three others… and Flo bending over Grandad.

The light dimmed. Molly looked up to where oval-shaped human eyes followed the fish around the bucket.

'That one's too big.'

'I couldn't catch the other one without netting b-both of them. They were swimming together.'

Human hands descended to grip the bigger fish firmly and lift it from the bucket.

'Whoa-ho! Slippery…'

'Look out, Andre.'

Molly heard a splash.

'S-stupid fish nearly threw itself in the shrubbery.'

'Can I have another little one then, instead of the big one. Ple-e-ase? Look, that baby white one with orange spots, there!'

The father said. 'This was the little one you wanted, wasn't it? Andre's been very clever to catch it.'

'But one fish isn't much company for Goldie.'

'All the fish would rather be in the pond, Beth, where they've got room to swim properly and grow big.'

'Ple-e-ase.'

Molly stopped trying to make sense of the grumblings and splashes outside the bucket and peered across its base to the three mirlings huddled there.

A small black fish plopped into the water to join the carroty one.

'That's it! No more! If you don't want these two, they can go back in the pond. They'll be better off there than in a bowl, and so would your Goldie.'

Andre's voice backed up his father. 'How would you like it if you c-could only ever walk round and round and round your room all the time?'

'Oh-h, all right. I'll just have these then.'

'Take them into the kitchen, Andre,' said the father, and the bucket rose.

Water slopped, and the sky moved.

Molly's world darkened as she left the sky behind. After much sloshing of water, the bucket came to rest on a table and the children's argument carried on into another room.

7 Nowhere to Hide

Surely, she would wake up any minute from this nightmare.

Flash had little to say now as he swam up the sheer sides of the bucket and around its walls, as if looking for somewhere to climb out.

Molly's gaze remained fixed on the black wall opposite. As her breathing steadied, her eyes followed the curve of the bucket. The other mirlings' faces were as blank as her thoughts, except for Flo, who was busy tending to Grandad.

It was lonely inside her head. She moved closer to the three who had been in the bucket before them.

'It's Sylva and Walter, isn't it? How did you get in here?'

Sylva stared as if she hadn't understood. The water quivered around her, and her lustrous scales had dulled to leaden grey. The youngest of the three answered – what was her name? Amy? Amber, that was it.

'We didn't see the net!' She shook her head earnestly. It was a large head for such a small body.

'We saw Flash and we were going to follow him to the prizegiving and there was a big "whoosh" and everything was black and we were dragged backwards.' She looked around her. 'And then we were here.'

Flash swam down, and Sylva's back straightened. She ran a hand through her silvery hair.

Walter dipped his head, as if saluting King Neptune. 'Hello. I'm Walter.' Sylva elbowed him. 'And this is Sylva.'

'Triffic to meet you,' Sylva simpered.

'And I'm Amber,' the little one added. 'Wally's my brother and Sylva's his girlfriend.'

'Don't talk rot, Amber.' Walter glanced nervously at Sylva whose trembling had stilled.

But her words still wobbled. 'What's ha-appening?' She gulped. 'They're going to pour us back into the pond, aren't they?'

Flo and Grandad joined them.

Flo understood humanspeak better than most. 'I think these fish are here to be k-kept indoors.'

'I think you're right, lass.' Grandad nodded. 'What we have to decide is if we want to go with them or take our chances in this bucket.'

'We have to stay together,' Sylva wailed. 'Walter?'

Flash ignored her. 'And our chances depend on what happens to the water after the fish are gone.' Seven pairs of eyes turned towards him. 'They might empty it back in the pond.' He looked to Grandad. 'But I think that's unlikely.'

The old mirling nodded. 'The sink's nearer for them to tip it down, or the nearest outside drain.'

Flash didn't elaborate on where drains went, but that didn't stop Molly's imagination following them down. Her throat tightened, and her stomach urged her to curl around it like a snail in its shell. All her familiar uncertainties and *what if*s were swept aside by the new fears flooding through her. Only the embarrassing spectacle of Sylva tipping into hysteria armed Molly against giving way to her own panic.

As Flo and Walter tried to calm Sylva and lead her away from Amber, Molly gazed up at the shapes circling the bucket and steadied her thoughts.

'Looks like we're safer staying with the fish then.'

The sky above the circling fish was white and strangely flat. Whatever sun flooded it with harsh light was out of their view.

Someone lowered a jug into the bucket. Water surged over its rim until the jug was full and rose again. The bucket darkened as a face blocked the light and oval eyes again followed the circling fish. Molly shrunk back against the side, glad of the darkness at the bottom of the bucket.

A small fishing net slid down the side and the orange fish was netted before they had time to plan.

Flash called, 'Come on!' and sped towards the rising net, seizing Flo's hand as he passed. He dragged her slight figure with him over the top of the net.

Eddy shouted, 'Flo,' and grabbed the net as it left the water. Flo thrust her arms through to grab his. 'Eddy, hold on.'

Sylva moaned.

Molly had no time to think. 'Walter, take Amber and Sylva and get above the fish so the net catches you on the way up.' Amber swayed like pondweed in a current. 'Amber, can you manage that?'

Amber nodded. 'I'll be all right. Come on Sylv.'

'We'll only get one chance.' Grandad started swimming.

The water darkened again. Molly powered upwards, linking arms with Grandad as she passed, to take him with her.

The net dipped.

The black fish flipped violently, hit the side, and swooped in terror around the bucket, pitching Molly and Grandad aside to drift like leaves to the bottom.

The net stilled while the fish calmed, giving Walter's group time to get in it and hang on.

When Molly sat up, sick and disoriented, she and Grandad were alone in the bucket.

The water was settling, but her stomach still churned, along with her thoughts.

What now?

There had always been someone in the pond to tell her what she ought to do, and to sort things out when she didn't do it.

Now, only Grandad sat beside her, limp and disoriented on the bottom of the bucket. And there were no more fish to catch.

The water darkened; this was it. Next stop, the drain. She waited to feel the bucket lift.

The jug descended again.

Grandad flipped over faster than she'd ever seen him move.

'Come on, lass. They might be topping up the fishbowl.' He launched from one knee.

Molly passed him, grabbing his hand on the way. Her tail drove as hard as she could to add to his thrust. The jug entered the bucket, and water flooded over its rim, washing Molly and Grandad with it, into safety.

Or not.

Grandad's thought reached Molly as they tumbled in the jug. 'I suppose they are emptying it in the bowl.'

Belatedly, they shared the realisation that the jug's water might still be destined for the drain, making the bucket lighter before it was carried to be emptied.

But what else could they have done?

They didn't wonder for long.

They tumbled from the jug into bright water with light all around, to be tossed again by the water that followed them.

Molly drifted to the bottom and waited, yet again, for her world to stop spinning around her. There was nowhere here for a mirling to hide.

The light on every side gave an illusion of space, but the bowl itself wasn't spacious. Even Grandad wouldn't get tired swimming across it. Or even walking across it.

The three fish circled, looking for a way out. The former dodger-fish suddenly flicked and swam across as if to frighten the glass out of his way, only turning at the last moment.

On the other side of the bowl, Flo was bending over Grandad; Molly could see from here how grey his gills were. Flash and Eddy circled with the fish while Walter's little group huddled against the curve of the base.

And there was nowhere to hide.

8   Planning Ahead

Flash still had nightmares about living behind glass walls in the pet shop, with faces staring in, and fingers pointing.

The faces here came even closer. When they pressed against the curved glass, they became demon faces.

The face that loomed most often belonged to the voice of Bethany. When she called out to the others, she didn't move away, and her voice shook the water.

While the other mirlings hugged the curved edges of the base, staying as still as sludge, he swam among the fish. In the pet shop he had kept his distance from other mirlings whose clumsiness might get him noticed.

Eddy swam up to join him. Flash showed him how to swim in the shadow of the fishes' fins, screened from human view.

Eddy had never been this close to humans. From the bottom of the pond, their faces hadn't looked so different from mirlings'.

'Their eyes are black in the middle like ours, but those brown rings are wider, and then they've got white bits.'

Flash didn't need Eddy telling him what they looked like. He'd hoped never to look into human eyes again.

'What are those flaps of skin that close over them? They're like frogs' lids, only thicker.'

Flash shrugged. It was bad enough in the pet shop, but these eyes stared from every side of the bowl.

It was a relief when the children left to go shopping with their father.

On his return, Father carried in a large rectangular glass tank like the ones the pet shop sold. The children followed bearing carrier bags.

Father pulled a bunch of waterweed from one bag and dropped it into the fishbowl. A band of metal held the stalks together. It sank to the bottom, and the bunch settled against the side of the bowl. The fish swam to investigate, but the mirlings dare not move while human eyes were watching.

Father directed the children to clear a shelf by the wall. With all eyes turned away from the bowl, Walter pushed Amber towards the clump of weed and Sylva darted in after her, followed by the other mirlings.

Flash had no wish to study the humans – most of his efforts had gone into hiding from them – but Eddy wouldn't drop the subject.

'Those lumps on their faces make their nostrils point down, and they don't ever close them. Maybe they can't. And their gills stick out too. All those sticky-out bits must slow down their swimming.'

Flash couldn't imagine them swimming. 'Maybe they're like the cat and don't want to get wet. They didn't come into the pond.'

'They'd need a bigger pond than ours. They're huge.'

'Their scales are tiny though.' He was, after all, the pond mirlings' expert on human faces. 'You can't see their scales, even this close.'

Eddy studied Bethany through the glass. 'They don't shimmer like ours either.'

Beth was equally fascinated by the fish, updating her family on every new discovery.

And she kept coming back.

The empty fish tank sat on the shelf against the nearest wall.

From the cover of the weed's top branches, Flash watched Father line the tank with gravel and place an ornamental bridge in the centre. He moved it further to one side before positioning large stones around it, which were rearranged several times.

Molly swam up to where Flash was viewing the transformation.

Walter followed, sent by Sylva to find out what was going on.

Father half-filled the tank with water, before pushing plant stems into the gravel around the stones. Finally, he reached behind the tank. Bubbles ascended from a tube at the back.

Bethany clapped. 'Daddy, that's cool. My fish will love living in there.'

Andre spoke from the doorway. 'They'd like the p-pond better.'

She ignored him. 'Can I put them in?'

'Not yet,' said Father. 'We have to leave it a day or two and let the tank settle.'

'Even though the water came from the p-pond?' asked Andre.

'It needs time for bacteria to build up in the filter.' His father checked the instruction booklet again.

'What are those b-black things on the glass?'

'Water snails,' Father tapped the glass and the tiny snail pulled in its feelers. 'The man in the pet shop said they help keep the tank clean.'

Bethany turned from the tank to the bowl.

Fish and mirlings scattered, only to find Andre watching from the other side.

'There's something else swimming around in there. Like b-bugs.'

'I expect they're from the pond. They won't do any harm. They'll be live food for the fish.'

'Can I feed the fish, Daddy?'

'Not yet. They'll be too stressed to eat after their move. Best to leave them for now.'

Bethany's nose pressed against the glass. 'I think those are baby fish. They're hiding.'

Andre's eyebrows drew together as he peered into the bowl. 'There's one! In the plant. It doesn't swim like the other fish. It's flipping up and d-down, instead of side to side.'

Father joined him.

After a moment, he shook his head. 'I can't see anything...' He turned to Bethany. 'Isn't it past your bedtime, young lady?'

Cries of protest followed him out of the kitchen as he sent Bethany to get ready for bed and Andre to finish his homework.

'That was close.'

Eddy could be relied on to state the obvious, thought Flash.

Molly, of course, could be relied on to give orders.

'We must stay hidden when they're in the kitchen. Even when they're not, we ought to get used to swimming on our sides, so we flip from side to side – like fry wriggling – instead of up and down.'

He wished he'd thought of that.

'But we'll be slower if we try to swim sideways. They'll have more time to spot us.'

'She's right though.' Grandad was getting his colour back. 'If they think we're baby fish, they're more likely to keep us when they move the fish to the tank.'

'But the safest thing is to stay in the weed,' Molly insisted, 'and not be seen at all'.

Flash had no intention of staying imprisoned in a bunch of weed. Imprisonment behind glass was bad enough.

It would be harder to escape the tank, with its straight walls and lid, but he could be gone before then. If he could get out of this bowl and down to the floor…

Mojo's water bowl would refresh his gills enough to get him through the door, or under it. How far was the pond from the house?

If it rained, there might be puddles. The grass would be wet.

It was a lot of ifs, but he had a day or two yet, to plan his escape.

9   Still

Even in the hottest weather, the pond would cool down at night, but here in the bowl, the water temperature hadn't changed.

Molly rested in the darkness. She sensed the others were awake too although they were all exhausted.

She listened to the bubbling of the tank nearby. This was a kind of torture to the mirlings drooping in the tepid stillness of the bowl. Mojo snored softly in his bed somewhere beneath them.

To take her mind off the gurgling tank, Molly asked Sylva and Walter how they'd met, and learned that their families were neighbours. They were more interested in learning about Flash, but Flash hadn't stayed to answer questions. He'd swum again to the surface and was circling the bowl, as if an escape route might have appeared since he last looked.

Flo turned to check on Grandad.

'How will we get home?' asked Walter, and three pairs of eyes fixed on Molly, as if she had an answer.

She shook her head. 'I wish I knew.'

Flo rejoined them. 'Grandad's dozing – at last.

Sylva looked puzzled. 'You all call him Grandad. Whose grandad is he?'

'N-nobody's,' replied Flo. 'N-none of us, anyway. He had a family before he was taken from the river, but he n-never settled with anyone from the pond.'

Molly had wondered why not but had never asked. Her grandmother had told of how the newcomer had kept to himself for years after he arrived. Few in the pond now were old enough to remember that far back.

As day came and the room lightened, two of the fish drifted up to swim around the bowl, but the carroty one – the former dodger-fish – remained on the bottom.

The parents appeared first. Bethany soon joined them in the kitchen.

'Daddy, Flipper isn't well,'

'Which one's Flipper, Beth?' asked her mother at the sink.

'Flipper's my flippy orange fish.'

'The one from the fairground?' asked her father, coming to the bowl.

'No, that's Goldie, he's more yellowy. The black one's Shadow. Can I feed them? Maybe Flipper's hungry.'

'Maybe he's homesick for his pond. Just a little pinch of food then, let's see if he comes up to feed.'

Coloured flakes appeared on the surface of the water. Their aroma drifted, reminding Molly how long it was since she'd last eaten. Two fish rose to the food, but the one Bethany called Flipper stayed on the bottom.

As the flakes were disturbed, some floated down through the water and one lodged in the weed. Molly waited until the humans turned away and broke off a chunk of flake to try it.

It tasted better than the pond pellets, which mirlings rarely bothered with. Pellets had to be hauled down from the surface and soaked to make them soft.

Molly and Flash dragged the flake deep into the weed, and Flash swam up to bring down another before she could tell him not to risk being seen.

The day dragged on, noisy and uncomfortable, as they huddled together in the weed. Molly became accustomed to the weight of fear she carried, her heart no longer quivering as if occupied by damselflies.

With no pump to carry away water for filtering, fish waste polluted the bowl. The warm, still water absorbed little oxygen from its tiny surface area, and the creatures inside breathed it quicker than it was replaced. Even Flash grew listless, and Sylva stopped asking unanswerable questions.

Goldie from the fairground was the only fish still swimming by the end of the day. She circled the bowl as the two pond fish rested on the bottom, gills pumping desperately.

'Daddy, Shadow's sick too. Are they going to die?'

Joel looked in and tapped on the glass. 'Probably.'

'Joel…' his father growled a warning. 'They're sleeping, honey. It's their bedtime, and yours too.'

'But their eyes are open.'

'Have you ever seen a fish with its eyes shut? Go get ready for bed. Mummy will come up for your story when you're ready. Joel! Homework.'

After the children had gone, their father spoke to his wife across the bowl in a low voice.

'Make it a long bedtime story. I'll move the fish over while she's out of the way. They'll have a chance to settle before the kids come tapping on the glass. It's got to be better than three of them in a bowl, whether the water's ready or not.'

'You said the pet shop gave you something to start up the filter bacteria,' said Mother. 'Didn't you use it?'

'I did, but it still says you should wait before you put fish in.'

'The water came from the pond anyway. It's not as if you used tap water.'

Flash had recklessly swum to the top of the bowl to listen, although Molly knew he couldn't understand much. She broadcast to the bowl. 'He's going to put the fish in the tank.'

Would he net them again? or tip the bowl in?

A hand reached in to pull out the bunch of weed. Molly felt Sylva's terror like a scream in her head as she clung instinctively to its fronds.

Above her, Walter's arms wrapped tightly around his sister and their branch. Flo linked an arm through Grandad's as they both clung on and Eddy tried to reach them. Molly didn't see if he made it before everything blurred as she left the water.

Without its buoyancy, her weight – slight as it was – dragged down the fine filaments she clung to. She tightened her grip. Was the weed heading for the tank, or the bin?

Her heartbeat pounded in her throat as they travelled through the air.

A splash beneath them was followed by a whoop and another splash. As the weed entered the tank, the colder water made her gasp, but she could see again. Eddy, Flo and Grandad were swimming for cover.

Flo won't have been brave enough to jump – Molly didn't think Flo's fingers would loosen their grip if her brain told them to. It was more likely Grandad lost his grip and slid off his branch, pulling Flo with him. The whoop will have been Eddy as he launched himself after them.

She had no time to adjust to the temperature change. Father's fingers moved to squeeze the weed's stalks into the gravel, and she dived into a neighbouring plant.

When she could breathe normally, she looked around for the others. Flo and Grandad waved from behind a stone.

Amber wriggled free of the weed as Walter backed out, releasing his grip on a branch, finger by finger.

'Amber, get back in the weed!'

'I'll be all right, Wally.'

'His name's Walter.' Sylva still clung to her branch.

Where was Flash?

10 Moving In

Flash had been at the top of the bowl when the hand appeared.

After a day skulking in the weed, the temptation to stretch his tail had been too strong to resist. Molly's warning reached him, but he was too far away to grab the weed before it left the tank. He'd have no trouble following the others on a fish

He thought he'd try riding Goldie, the fairground fish, but she had been spooked by the hand in the water and wasn't about to suffer a mirling on her back.

After Goldie threw him, he dropped instead to the pond fish at the bottom.

A plastic bag appeared at the surface. Water flowed in, and it was removed.

The tiny net easily scooped up the lethargic pond fish and Flash, tucked behind the pectoral fin of the black one lately named Shadow.

The fish were emptied into the water-filled bag, which now rested in a jug on the table.

He settled at the bottom of the bag until Goldie joined them and the bag was tied at the top to be floated in the tank.

Eddy was first up to investigate. 'Are you OK, mate? Can you get out of there?'

Flash waved out and grinned at Eddy as Molly joined them.

'He doesn't look particularly worried.' She eyed him through the bag. 'You've seen this before, haven't you?'

He would have liked to see Flo out there worrying too, but it was Walter who swam up next. 'The man's gone. What's Flash doing in there?'

He relented. 'Don't worry, Walt. He'll be back to let us out when our water temperature's the same as the tank's. It's what they did in the pet shop.'

Molly nodded. 'The cold water did make us gasp. Grandad's still gasping.'

That would be where Flo was, looking after Grandad.

Eddy stayed to make faces through the bag, and Flash was glad of the company. It helped pass the time and stopped him thinking of the pet shop.

When the kitchen light came on, Eddy hid in the weed while Father untied the bag and let its water mingle with the tank's. Flash wanted to shoot out to freedom but held back and tucked himself under Shadow's fin.

It took all his self-control. The carroty Flipper rallied in the fresher water and swam a short way before settling on the gravel, but Shadow didn't swim out. Father shook her from the bag when he pulled it from the water, and the black fish sank to the gravel floor.

At the bottom of the tank, Flash left Shadow's shelter and joined the other mirlings where they had gathered behind a stone.

He was too exhausted to stay awake for long. The others were already asleep when he gave up trying and slept as if he were safe back in the pond.

Molly was relieved to be out of the bowl and no longer exposed on every side.

Molly told Amber they should stay out of sight at the back when the family were in the kitchen. She hoped the others were taking notice.

Shadow roused herself from the gravel as the morning brightened, and Molly's spirits lifted too. She recognised the little black fish as one of last season's hatchlings. Bethany was the first of the family to notice Shadow's revival and shrieked the news to the rest of the house.

Even with so many places to hide, Molly was uncomfortable with the attention the tank received. It wasn't only Bethany; Andre had resumed his search for the baby fish that didn't swim like other fish. He would stare into the tank until the whites of his eyes reddened, and even Flash was careful to stay out of sight.

Flo confided to Molly that she quite liked Andre, even if he was human. 'But his eyes are m-making me nervous. I wish he'd stop looking for us.'

But as time passed, the children spent less time staring into the tank. Molly began to relax and take in her surroundings.

When evening came, the family moved into another room. Venturing to the front of the tank, Molly's eyes were drawn to the window, still bright in the kitchen's half-light.

She imagined herself out there, watching through the water as the sky darkened, but the longing became too much to bear. Turning away, she saw other eyes reflecting the window's light.

'This would be a good time to practise swimming on our sides so that our swim thrusts look more fishlike.'

Flash rolled his eyes and shook his head sadly.

She vowed to keep her thoughts to herself in future and swam out to put as much distance between them as the tank allowed.

She found swimming on her side was easy in short bursts but keeping it up confused her sense of direction.

Grandad couldn't get the hang of it at all, but he didn't swim much anyway. The others were soon swimming almost as fast on their good side as they did normally.

Flash, of course, swam equally well on either side, although he clearly resented being told to by Molly.

But if one of them were spotted, it would put them all at risk.

At least now they could breathe properly and recover.

Each had their own way of settling in.

Flash continued to swim with the fish, recklessly risking discovery and leading Eddy into danger with him. Grandad took a long time to recover from the bowl, and Flo spent much of her time fussing over him. Amber wanted to explore everything. She tired quickly, but Wally was still hard-pressed to keep track of her.

Flo prepared meals for everyone and made sure Grandad ate something. Flash and Eddy scavenged for food near the surface and brought their findings to the clearing at the back of the tank which Flo had appropriated as galley. Two hollows fashioned among the stems of the screening plants allowed Grandad to rest nearby during the day, and Flo to be on hand at night when everyone slept.

Molly gathered fallen flake and harvested new shoots, ensuring she left enough shoots to provide them with leaves later. n.

Sylva had discovered a dark area of the glass wall that threw back her reflection. Before breakfast each morning she could be found there, combing out her hair and arranging her armlets and necklaces of plaited grasses. Neither Walter nor Flash seemed to notice her efforts.

Molly had never felt so alone. She missed the sky.

11 Homemaking

'Bother and blast!'

Sylva joined them for breakfast wearing a petulant frown. She threw a length of fine cord onto the gravel.

'My favourite necklace is broken.'

Flo picked it up and examined the break.

'I might be able to mend that for you.'

'Can you do that – mend broken cords?'

'Well, Grandad's the expert.' Flo passed him the necklace to examine.

'There in't any of these stems in the tank.' He pulled down a branch of the nearest plant to examine. 'But I'm sure these'll strip down alright.'

He turned his attention back to the necklace. 'Not worth mending this one though. Look, it's breaking up here… and here.' He handed it back to Sylva. 'It's probably time to give up with this one and make a new one.'

'Me?'

This was clearly an alien concept to Sylva.

'Or I can make you one if you like?'

'No – I'd like to do it. Can you teach me?'

Flo was interested too.

'I'd like to know how to strip the stems. I only ever plaited blanketweed when you taught us before.'

'Ay. Well, you won't be finding any of that here, lass. Blanketweed needs sunlight. We'll go hunt out suitable stems after breakfast, shall we? Once the kiddies out there are off to school. We don't want to be stripping away our screening at the back here.'

'If you show me what to collect, we can gather stems for you,' offered Walter. 'Can't we Amber?'

Amber nodded enthusiastically. Molly couldn't imagine her dragging long stems across the pond floor, but Eddy volunteered to help.

Grandad had spoken more that morning than since they arrived in the tank. Flo beamed her approval to Sylva.

And what else was there to do in this glass box?

'Count me in with your lessons, Grandad,' added Molly. 'I could do with the practice.'

After breakfast, she went to her sleeping hollow among the stems to tidy it while waiting for the children to leave for school. The black goldfish drifted after her.

In the pond, the fish had been part of the landscape – an annoying part during spawning season. In the tank, she got to know them better.

Goldie the fairground fish ignored the mirlings. She bullied the other fish if they got in her way and swam doggedly around the tank all day on her own. Flipper, the dodger-fish, was angry with the world and best avoided, but the black one Beth had named Shadow was an affectionate little fish.

Shadow had taken to Molly and would swim down to nudge her for attention. When the kitchen light went out at night, the little fish settled on the gravel near Molly's bed.

Although she rarely swam far from cover, Molly felt safe swimming under Shadow's fin, their darkness merging. She often shared her thoughts with the black fish. Their conversations were rather one-sided. Shadow didn't understand a ripple of them but wouldn't leak them to the other mirlings.

Nobody spoke of the pond.

Molly had tried talking to Grandad. He would shake his head sadly.

'What do I know about fish tanks, lass?' And he withdrew again into his own thoughts.

His colour had returned. He hadn't regained his former chirpiness but when the humans were away at work and school, he would look out into the empty kitchen and sometimes sound like the Grandad they'd known in the pond.

'You see more if you stay still,' he pointed out one day. 'You don't notice things when you're zooming around like mayflies.'

Typically, Flash and Eddy weren't around to hear it, but Amber was. For the rest of the afternoon she sat humming to herself as she watched a water snail creep up the tank wall. She could have concealed herself better, but Molly thought it had to be safer than trailing around after Eddy and Flash.

Whenever Eddy called, 'Come for a swim, kid,' Amber would follow. Most of the time, Walter had no idea where his sister was.

He had tried to stop her swimming off until Eddy suggested he come too. Walter's eyes had brightened at the invitation, but Sylva was close at hand to remind him of some chore she'd asked him to do.

Amber had sung out, 'I'll be all right, Wal,' as she paddled after Eddy.

Molly wasn't convinced. Walking or swimming, Amber weaved from side to side as if buffeted by currents no-one else could feel. She looked as if a careless tail could flip her out of the water.

But Molly wasn't their mother. Amber wasn't her responsibility, and Wally didn't try to stop her again. Nevertheless, she was reassured to see Eddy waiting for Amber to catch them up and staying with her whenever Flash amused himself dive-bombing the goldfish.

What would happen if the humans saw them?

Come to that, what would happen if they didn't? Would they be stuck here for the rest of their lives? She'd formed no plans for her life, but she had imagined her aimless future would be in the pond.

The next time she saw Amber and Eddy swimming up to meet Flash, she couldn't stop herself reminding them to be careful.

She was beginning to sound like her mother.

One afternoon the children's father brought home a carrier bag. It bore a drawing of a strange fish, with oversized fins and a smile that Molly thought wasn't at all fishlike.

'You've been to the pet shop again,' said his wife.

'It's a proper aquarium shop near work,' he said. 'I just went in to have a look around.' He showed her a small box. 'These are brine shrimps. A treat for the fish.'

He'd never fed those to the pond fish. Molly wondered how they'd taste.

He dipped into the carrier again and brought out a clear bag of water. In it wriggled two fat fish with big fins. One fish was orange and white, the other, black.

'These fantails are better for an indoor aquarium.' He lifted the lid of the tank and floated the bag on the water.

His wife came to look at the fish in the bag, close enough for Molly to hear the strange tutting sound she made. As she moved back, she raised her eyes to the ceiling, but Molly couldn't see what she was looking at.

Father took out another clear bag, this time with plants in. Mother shook her head and went back to the cooker while he took out the last item: a roll of paper. Unrolled, it became a picture of rocks and pond plants, which he slid behind the tank and fastened to the edges.

Something about the dark waterscape was reassuring. Molly felt less exposed, even though Father's hand invaded the tank several more times while she watched from under the bridge. He removed any clumps of waterweed that were looking ragged and positioned the new plants.

After he'd admired his handiwork and taken his tea into the other room, the mirlings discovered that one of the new plants tasted good, and that two brine shrimps made a meal for them all. In fact, the dried delicacies lasted well, becoming softer and less salty after a soak in the tank. Along with algae scraped from the stones, they were a welcome addition to their diet on the days Mother forgot to feed flake to the fish.

Father remarked one day that baby fish would be big enough to spot by now if they were still alive and said they had probably been eaten by the goldfish. To Molly's relief, Andre gave up his search for them.

To cheer the boy up, Father revisited the aquarium shop and arrived home with a bag of small silvery fish that darted together around the aquarium like a single shape-shifting fish. Father told the children they were mountain minnows.

The minnows reminded Molly of the clouds of birds that flocked across the sky together at the end of summer, high over the cooling pond.

The tasks of feeding and tank cleaning had passed to Mother, since Father sometimes worked away for several days. It was she who cleaned the filter every week and scraped algae from the tank walls although, fortunately, she didn't scrub algae from the stones.

It was she who vacuumed the gravel with a syphon – a fat rigid tube that attached to a thinner flexible one and tumbled the gravel, sucking out debris.

The mirlings learned to keep their distance from this.

It was, of course, Eddy who ventured too close to the fat tube and was sucked inside with the gravel. Horrified, they watched him tumble with the stones before being syphoned up the narrow tube and out of sight.

Flo and Amber were inconsolable.

Flash swam up in a bid to discover where Eddy had gone. Molly felt useless.

Mother finished vacuuming and took the bucket to the sink, but Flash reported no sign of Eddy.

All Molly could do was listen as Flo assured Amber that of course Eddy would find a way back to them. Unless he managed to find his way back to the pond.

Flo's eyes met Molly's over Amber's head, seeking similar reassurance that Molly wished she could offer.

Mother returned later to top up their water level. Molly heard a whoop from Flash as Eddy was unceremoniously poured back into the tank.

'I thought I was done for,' he admitted when he had got his thoughts in order.

'I shot out of the tube into a bucket where I couldn't breathe properly. I'd had the water knocked out of me by the tumbling, and the bucket was thick with muck sucked out of the gravel.

'Breathing got easier as the sludge settled at the bottom. I was sitting on it, certain I was about to become a snack for a sewer rat, when the bucket started to tip. I realised the top layer of cleared water was being tipped into a plastic bowl.'

He shuddered. 'I couldn't be sure the water would go back in the tank, but I knew the muck wouldn't, so I swam for it.'

After that, Molly looked for Amber whenever the vacuum tube appeared, but Eddy was always there before her. She would hear his, 'Come on, kid,' and she knew Amber would be safe away from the vacuum.

She only hoped Flash's fan club were keeping well hidden from Mother while she vacuumed. They didn't want Andre resuming his hatchling hunts.

12 Dreams

Flash hadn't told anyone about the nightmares he had brought with him to the pond.

Every night, he dreamed of being back in the pet shop. Each morning, the open sky rippling above the pond would reassure him that those days were over.

The nightmares became less frequent. By the week of the tournament, they had stopped altogether and didn't return, even after the encounter with the cat shook his confidence.

And he had still won the longshot crown. If it weren't for that cat, he would have won the tournament outright. He had been looking forward to wearing his prize, seeing his future carved in the swirls and peaks of Grandad's reed crown.

He wondered what had happened to those prizes.

Instead of sporting a crown, he was here, reliving the nightmare of his past.

In place of the distant, reassuring sky, a flat ceiling again bore down on him. He understood Flipper's frustration, powering through the water only to meet his own reflection in the glass.

Unlike Flipper, the new fantails bustled happily around the tank. They too roused depressing memories of the pet shop, despite their cheerful appearance. The neighbouring display tank had been busy with them.

Bethany had named the white and orange one, Finny and the piebald male, Fanny. The useless things didn't buck like Flipper, but they were too wriggly for Amber to ride.

Grandad had aged since leaving the pond. Flo spent what time she could with him and hardly noticed when Flash was around.

She always had fussed over Eddy, but now she took Amber into her shoal. She insisted they all come together for meals, so she could ensure that the weakest had their share and gently bully them until they ate.

Flash didn't mind. Some days, it was the only time he saw her. He was usually first in the galley for breakfast.

One morning, he arrived to find Wally already there, helping Flo.

Sylva appeared, hair uncombed, clearly unhappy with this development. She always found tasks to keep Walter under her eye in the hollow she had claimed for the three of them. Either the gravel needed cleaning to discourage goldfish from rooting in it – Mother didn't vacuum near the plants for fear of dislodging them – or else the vacuum had strayed too close, and Wal was expected to deal with the resulting chaos.

But Wally still found time to help Flo, and he was a fast learner. He learned to identify plants that were turning sour, or flake that was about to grow mould, and his leaf patties were the smoothest any of them had tasted.

This particular morning, the results of their cord plaiting lessons had to be moved aside to make space for breakfast.

'Is your blade strong enough to chop this plant back, Grandad?' asked Flo. 'There's space on the other side that could join up with this space and we'd have more room to do things together.'

Needless to say, moaning Molly had an objection.

'Would the plant be too thin to hide us if we chopped half of it away?'

Flash picked up one of the cords that had been moved aside. It was uneven, thick and knobbly, but strong.

'We could use this stronger rope to move it instead. If we all help to pull, we can make a channel in the gravel to drag the plant along and bring it into line with the other plants. Can you make more of this?'

'That's our Moll's.' Grandad nodded at Molly. 'We need more, lass."

'I can make more.' Molly looked surprised, but gratified.

'What a good idea, Flash,' simpered Sylva. 'Your plaiting is good for something after all, Molly.'

No doubt, Sylva had also seen the advantages of more people joining Flo and Wally in the galley.

Flash helped, taking the opportunity to learn how to roughly plait rope with Molly while the others sliced stems and prepared them. After a few days there was enough cord to shift the plant and double their galley space.

When the plant had been moved, while the others were pushing gravel into the trench behind it, Flash rolled up the cord and stowed it safe.

He might be able to use it.

Sylva still haunted the galley whenever Wally was there. The impression Flash got was that she wasn't much help, but Flo was happy to leave the two of them in charge of things when Molly started seeking her out for a chat.

Flash wondered what new directives Molly was cooking up now.

The tank seemed safe, but he was homesick for the community he had belonged to so briefly in the pond.

He missed his team; he missed his supporters; he missed mirlings he hadn't met yet. He missed the challenges of the pump and yearned for the freedom to swim as far and as fast as he could.

He missed the sky.

It was Flo who dared to raise the question one day, while they were feasting on fern leaves and a brine shrimp that he had seized almost from the mouth of a fantail.

'Do you think we'll ever g-go back?'

Flo was braver than the others gave her credit for.

Grandad's eyes were grey as winter skies.

'I've learned there's nothing gained by living in the past. Think of the past as water that's flowed under the bridge and gone.'

Sylva eyed the ornamental bridge, confusion creasing her brow. Flash wondered how many of them understood Grandad's image of bridges *over* water. In the pond, water didn't flow away, never to return, as it did in the river. It was pumped through a filter and came back via the waterfall.

But Grandad had never forgotten his other life. And here he was, dragged again from the water he had learned to call home.

'You must do best you can, lass, with what you've got now. You'll never survive if you're always looking back.'

Flash registered Grandad's words. Shouldn't that be, *we* must do the best we can, or *we'll* never survive?

'Never say never, Grandad. You told us that, remember?'

Amber stopped humming to herself and looked up from her shrimp.

'I like it here.'

Flash wondered if Amber had been bullied in the pond.

Sylva stopped eating. 'We have to stay together.' Panic in her eyes, she looked to Walter for support. 'It's better we all stay safe here, isn't it, Walter?'

'It's nice enough here.' He seemed unsure, but willing to be convinced. 'I suppose.'

Grandad's quiet thought was almost lost. 'It in't home.'

Flash had allowed himself to think Grandad was comfortable here.

The water was warmer than the pond, food appeared daily and there wasn't far to walk.

He hadn't complained. The bronze colour had returned to his skin, if not his eyes, and he seemed recovered from the goldfish bowl, but something was missing.

In the pond his body had been stiff and slow, but his thoughts had been as lively as any of them.

Eddy caught Flash's eye before facing Flo with an apologetic expression.

'We've been thinking about ways to get home.'

His eyes dropped to his hand, where a finger picked at a loose scale. 'We wouldn't have gone without you, but we didn't want to get your hopes up by saying anything.'

'Hopes?' Sylva looked from Eddy to Flo, and then to Grandad.

Flash steeled himself for Molly's disapproval. He had been keeping out of her way. They only crossed paths at mealtimes, which they could just manage without sniping at each other.

Now Flo was smiling at Eddy's discomfort.

'Molly and I have been talking about it too. We didn't mention it because it seems so… impossible.'

Sylva was speechless, which was a nice change.

Grandad looked chirpier than he had for ages.

'Now don't you youngsters try anything daft.' He paused. 'But if we do come up with anything *that we all agree on*,' he looked around with a stern expression, 'don't expect me to tag along and hold you back.'

They all felt Flo's shock.

Eddy protested. 'Don't talk daft, old mir. We're not going anywhere without you.'

'We're not going anywhere at all,' Molly added quietly.

'That's all right, then.' Sylva ended the discussion. 'Can someone pass me some more of that shrimp?'

The school holidays arrived, and the children were around all day. Every day.

Flash learned to understand humanspeak as well as the pond mirlings did.

Andre caught sight of Sylva one morning as she swam back into the weed from her morning reflection. He decided the fish must have spawned, not realising how unlikely that was, and resumed his hatchling hunts.

Father set up a piece of equipment under the lid of the tank. All night, it ticked quietly above them. In the morning it made a whirring sound and flakes fell from it to the water.

That morning, the family were up early and buzzing around the kitchen. Children ran in and out, getting in their parents' way, and Father checked the new feeder.

'That does the job! The first compartment's empty and the wheel's moved around. We won't have to worry about the fish starving while we're away.'

'Oh, bother!' said Mother. 'I meant to vacuum the aquarium yesterday and clean the filter. What with the packing and everything, I didn't get around to it.'

'I'm sure it'll be fine. Do it when we get back.'

'Along with the unpacking and the washing and the ironing, you mean?'

'*I'll* do it when we get back.' Father's voice remained cheerful as the bustle rose to a crescendo.

The front door closed, and the kitchen was quiet.

13 Holiday

It was quiet for days.

And days…

The mirlings were free to swim whenever they wanted without keeping watch for humans.

The automated feeder dispensed more flake than the fish needed. The overfed fish produced more waste, and uneaten flake fell into the gravel to rot.

Eddy, Flash and Grandad spent ages discussing the fate of the watery murk that Mother syphoned out of the gravel.

So did Molly, Flo and Grandad. Flash learned this from Sylva, who had a knack of joining conversations when you thought she wasn't in range.

Sylva also reported that Molly was becoming reconciled to life in the tank, since these 'what if…' sessions were usually brought back to reality by Grandad's infuriating common-sense. 'They in't going to pour that muck in the pond, though, are they.'

And yet… this was the only way anyone had escaped the tank since their arrival. They could surely think of a way to escape the bucket before being emptied down the drain.

Whenever Sylva tuned in on an escape committee, she would repeat, 'We have to stay together,' but her mantra had lost its urgency. After hearing their unlikely suggestions, she no longer seemed afraid that anyone would be foolhardy enough to risk any of them.

A sheet of clear plastic rested on a rim at the top of the tank. Two holes had been cut in this thin plastic, for the pump's wiring to pass through and the flake to drop from the new feeder.

Flash could reach this clear sheet by climbing up the pump's tube and pulling himself onto the plastic. When the others were asleep, he brought himself up here to practice holding his breath for long periods.

Above this plastic, a lid of thicker black plastic rested, like a rectangular hat, on the top of the tank. This had holes at each end to accommodate whatever wiring was needed to operate lights, pumps and other equipment. Their tank had only the pump and the fish-feeder, so there was plenty of space for a mirling to squeeze through to the outside world.

Might an exceptionally fit mirling with a rope be able to reach the floor?

Once he reached the shelf at the bottom of the tank, how could he untie his rope from the top of the tank? He would need a second rope.

Where could he secure his rope from the shelf for the drop to the floor?

How long must he hold his breath to reach the shelf, attach the rope, slide to the floor, and run to Mojo's bowl?

How much more rope would he need?

On the third day, the water began to taste... sharp. It caught in Flash's throat when swimming. He tried not to take in too much at once, so that it could pass through his gills without stinging.

When the feeder stopped working, fish looked for other food, nibbling at the leaves that Flash wanted to take for Flo and stripping plants that helped oxygenate the water. They rooted for rotting food in the gravel and sent muck drifting back up into the tank.

The polluted water was unpleasant to breathe and held less oxygen, so Flash had to take more of the foul stuff through his gills to get enough. He gave up practising holding his breath.

The pond fish grew sluggish. The black one stayed close to Molly; he wondered if she was feeding it. Grandad's bronze took on a grey hue.

Amber's recent rosy glow from her swimming sessions faded to a watery mustard colour. Her new-found energy was quickly drained. Flash heard panic in Walter's protests.

'I told you, you're not strong enough to go off swimming with Eddy.'

'The exercise is good for us,' Eddy insisted, 'and Flash carries her when she's tired.'

'Don't worry, Walt,' added Flash. 'We'll look after her.'

Sylva bristled. 'His name's Walter.'

'I quite like Walt,' came the quiet protest.

Amber reassured her brother. 'I'll be alright, Walt.'

By day five, they were all drooping. Walter turned to Flo for help, and she installed Amber beside Grandad, who entertained her with his tales of the river while Flo fussed over them both.

Walt stayed close to Amber's side and Sylva had to be there too, so the sickbeds became a gathering point.

Amber and Eddy played fivestones, and she laughed at Eddy's awful jokes, even though she had to stop to catch her breath.

The day after that, none of them were laughing.

Flash foraged for what food he could find, and Molly prepared it in silence as Flo tried not to make it obvious that she, too, was drooping.

There must be something he could do.

If only he could get his brain working properly to think what it was.

Little was moving in the tank when the family arrived home. Fish hung listlessly in the water or rested on the gravel. Flash crawled into cover as the children bounded into the kitchen. He had stopped looking out for humans.

Andre paused by the tank. 'What's that smell?'

'Yeuch!'

'It's the fish tank.'

Father lifted the tank's lid.

'It's the fish food. It's got damp and gummed up the holes so the flake can't drop.'

'Well, get rid of it,' said Mother. 'And if the tank still smells you'll need to clean the gravel. And the filter.'

Mother had become as knowledgeable as Father since taking over its maintenance.

'It must be condensation,' said Father. 'Perhaps we should have left the lid open.'

'A partial water change would help,' Mother added with satisfaction in her voice. 'I'll be unpacking the suitcases.'

Flash watched from a scraggy patch of weed as Father vacuumed the gravel. The fish had eaten much of the weed, and its stripped stalks offered little cover, but he kept very still. Father was too preoccupied to notice him. Mother hummed to herself on the other side of the kitchen as she fed armfuls of clothes into the washing machine.

Flash noticed more from his stationary post than he did when swimming around the tank. He noticed plants drooping on the windowsill, and Mojo sneaking off with a sock from the washing pile. He noticed the drawers under the shelf whose round handles would support a cord if he could clamber down to knot its end.

Father poured in fresh water from the pond to replace the water vacuumed out with the sludge, and Flash felt a wave of nostalgia as he breathed in the smells of the pond.

Goldie rose from the gravel and flexed her tail, followed by the fantails and Flipper.

Eddy swam up to join Flash, his homesickness seeping into the water around him.

'You don't want to go down there,' he warned. 'Molly started turning the gravel under the plants so the muck would get vacuumed away with the rest. Now Sylva's moaning at Wally for not getting theirs cleared before Father finished vaccuming.'

'How did Molly get the muck out for collecting? Wasn't she afraid of being seen?'

'Father had to go off a few times to empty the bucket. He's replaced a lot of water.'

In silence, they enjoyed the lingering traces of the pond.

Eddy asked, 'Why do you dislike Molly so much?' and his answer came without thinking.

'Because she's always right.'

Eddy paused to consider. 'She doesn't really believe that, Flash. Flo says Molly only ever wanted a quiet life in the pond. Unnoticed. She wants to keep us safe.'

'So does Grandad, but he doesn't tell everyone what they should be doing. She's like a mosquito buzzing in the background.'

The annoying thing was, Molly *was* right – about staying out of sight, about keeping their gravel clean, about everything.

Even more annoying was that people listened to her.

He had worked hard to recruit his team and lead them to victory. OK, some useless shooters had gone over to Molly. He'd told himself those weren't worth worrying about. Why, then, did it matter?

She had made no effort to impose leadership but, somehow, Eddy's success was supposed to be due to her too.

He groaned. 'What's the point of all these safety instructions anyway when there's so much that we can't influence. What can *we* do if one of Beth's friends pours in too much flake, or the pump stops working, or the glass breaks…?'

Flash took a breath and waited for the oxygenated water to cool his frustration.

'There's precisely nothing we can do to help ourselves. We can't turn on the pump or vacuum the muck away. And we can't get everyone out of here.'

14 Happy New Year

Next morning, when the day lightened, Shadow was floating on her side at the top of the tank, gills pulsing desperately. Molly swam up to her, but all she could do was stroke the fish's scales and try to comfort her.

When Mother came downstairs, she saw the black fish bobbing against the glass wall. Molly swam into the highest branches of weed as Mother scooped water from the tank, emptying several mugfuls into a basin. She fished out Shadow in the same way, pouring her too into the basin. Molly felt empty inside as Mother took Shadow away. She couldn't even be with her, but perhaps the humans could help the fish.

Father said to hide the bowl under the sink before the children came down for breakfast. He didn't want Bethany to see it before school.

When they had all left, Mother took the basin from the cupboard, and put it on the worktop, by the sink.

Molly watched all morning from the top of the weed, her hopes rising every time Mother checked the bowl. Flash and Eddy avoided her, but Amber came to watch with her for a while.

The last time Mother peered into the bowl, she prodded Shadow with a spoon handle before carrying the basin out of the kitchen.

Molly waited. The hollow feeling had turned into a dull ache around her middle

The children came home from school.

Father came home from work. Mother shook her head at him. Nothing was said.

Molly returned to the floor of the tank.

Bethany didn't notice that Shadow was gone.

More weeks passed.

The mirlings recovered from the family's holiday.

Each shelter among the plants began to reflect the character of its occupant, with emergency snacks, decorative bangles or belts, and amusingly shaped shards of gravel.

The children brought more friends to see the tank, and the mirlings learned humans weren't all the same colour after all, although their range was limited. They brightened their unexciting browns and pinks and beiges with coverings of different colours which they changed often and were rarely seen without.

Father often came home with more bags from the aquarium shop.

One day he brought a piece of driftwood with a fernlike plant growing out of it which was soft to eat straight from the stem.

On another day he brought a plant with flat leaves which the fish kept dislodging when they rooted in the gravel. It grew just as well drifting on the water and made an excellent lookout point when the family were around.

Her gills ached when she remembered Shadow. No other fish could replace her. The fantails were cheerful, busy little bodies, bustling around the tank. They were always pleased to see her – they were pleased to see anyone. Molly had the impression they forgot about mirlings as soon as they swam up and lost sight of them.

The minnows swooped around the tank together, like those birds that flocked across the sky in swarms that Father had called starlings. Molly missed the birds.

She missed the sky.

Most of the time, the tank was well maintained, and the water rich with oxygen; although it began to stale if they were overdue for a vacuum and water-change. She'd become used to the hum of the pump vibrating in the background: a reassurance that all was well. Food was plentiful and, once the humans stopped staring at them, life was stress free.

Nothing was expected of her. There was no new-laid spawn to chase the fish from and no freshly hatched fry to shepherd into cover. Her parents weren't forever nagging or hauling her off to visit relations.

She missed them.

She wondered if the Misfits were still reed-shooting. The team's easy acceptance of her had fed her confidence, which wasn't as strong as others supposed. People assumed she was capable of things that Molly herself wasn't so sure about.

The Misfits had been fun, though. It had worked. She was grateful to Grandad for pushing her to do it.

Flo usually had people around her, but they found time to chat now Grandad was stronger. Nobody spoke again about leaving the tank and Sylva had relaxed, even telling Molly what a 'triffic' job she was doing. (What job?)

Lately, Sylva had sought out Molly, who found her hard to warm to. They had little in common and Molly wasn't good at small talk. Sylva would babble on anyway, not noticing the lack of response

Walt had reconciled to having his little sister around all the time, and Amber's cheerful humming became a background to their daily activities, like the whirring of the pump.

Amber was a cheery soul even when ill, which was a lot of the time. Her happiest days were the ones when Molly saw Eddy beckon her away for a game of fish-chase as the morning lightened, before Walt or Sylva had time to tell her how ill she looked.

More time passed.

'Why do all the shop signs say, "Back to School"? We've only just broken up.'

'I picked up a couple more fantails while I was in the pet shop.'

'Go check your bags, kids. Make sure you've got everything you need for school next week.'

'The fish don't seem very lively. Have you cleaned the gravel lately?'

'Don't go making plans to meet your school friends at half term. We're going to visit Aunt Felicia.'

'The fish look fine. A week without food hasn't done them any harm. That auto-feeder was a waste of money.'

'Not more fish, Henry. You went to the pet shop for Mojo's flea shampoo.'

Each morning, the window lightened a little later and darkened earlier in the afternoon. In the hours between, the sky outside the window was mostly grey.

On days when the sun shone, it touched the window briefly before the house cast its shadow across the garden. It wasn't long before frosted spiderwebs in the window corners and sparkling branches on a nearby tree heralded midwinter in the outside world. In the pond, they would be settling around the lower levels of the deep end, where the water never froze, for deep winter's sleep.

Here, in the tank, a nearby radiator ensured that the temperature was always summer, whatever the window told them.

'Happy New Year, everyone!'

Unfamiliar humans passed through the kitchen. Some stopped to look at the fish.

Molly hid.

Even Flash was nowhere visible.

At one point the guests crowded into the other room and began chanting. There was a cheer and loud bangs, followed by everyone singing and then more bangs.

After the bangs stopped, the children went to bed, and the adults carried on without them.

Molly enjoyed listening in to conversations. It annoyed her when people moved out of hearing halfway through.

'You should try tropical fish, Abby. They're more colourful. You've got everything you need here except a water heater.'

'Please don't suggest that to Henry. All this was only set up because Beth won a goldfish at the fair and wouldn't put it in the pond. Henry got all enthusiastic, reading up about aquariums and fish diseases, but I'll give you three guesses who gets to pull out the dead ones and clean the tank.'

The women moved away laughing.

Molly couldn't see what was funny about dead fish, but sometimes she wasn't sure she'd understood properly.

On the day after all the people came, the kitchen lights went out and the bubbles stopped. Molly hardly noticed the constant whirr of the pump now, but she noticed when it fell silent.

Joel wailed a protest from the other room. 'Mum, the TV's gone off!'

'Henry! Can you check the fuse box? Andre, look and see if the neighbours' lights are out too.'

'I think so, Mum. I can't see any lights on anywhere. It must be a p-power cut.'

The children appeared in the kitchen. 'We're missing the film.'

The lights came on again, accompanied by beeps and pings from around the kitchen. The children were summoned by the sound of the television.

But Molly didn't hear the whirring start up again. And the bubbles hadn't come back.

Next morning, when Mother fed the fish, she didn't notice the pump was still off.

None of the family noticed.

They went out early to the sales and returned in darkness, carrying many bags. Mother took her bags upstairs. The children took theirs into the living room. Father joined them to watch television.

With a crowded tank and no pump to circulate the water, oxygen levels were low. Nobody was likely notice until Mother fed the fish again in the morning. Molly struggled to think.

This time they had to do something.

15 Doing Something

Flo came to find Molly.

'I'm worried about Grandad. He's gone a funny colour, and his breathing's sort of… gurgly. Amber's gasping again, and Eddy's trying to be tough, but he isn't looking good either.' She pushed back wisps of hair from her eyes. 'I don't know how long he'll hold out if the water gets worse.'

Flo didn't mention how she felt herself, but her usual pearly sheen had a grey tinge, and her gills were an unpleasant shade of pink.

Sylva brought an armful of weed, trimmed from her home plant. 'I don't suppose any of us feel like eating, but this is in case anyone gets hungry. Not as tempting as Walter's triffic leaf patties.'

Sylva preened as if she'd taught him herself.

Flo hardly noticed her. 'The children are busy with their new clothes and their Christmas toys. Mother is busy running around after them. Somehow we have to make them look at the tank.'

Flash had joined them with Eddy trailing behind. Molly turned to them.

'Flo's right. We have to make the humans look twice and notice something's wrong. Any ideas?'

'Other than dancing a jig at the front of the tank, you mean?' Flash turned away.

'I don't think they'd notice.' Eddy looked drained.

'Andre m-might.'

Flash folded his arms across his chest. 'We can show them a pile of dead fish if it goes on much longer.'

'N-not if we're dead M-mirlings, we can't.'

Molly could taste Flo's anger.

Eddy put a comforting arm around his sister, but in the next breath he was leaning on her.

Flo looked from Flash to Molly. 'We could build a pile of *something* though, couldn't we?'

Flo's thinking was muzzy, but her eyes expected Molly to understand. An image surfaced.

'Good thinking, Flo.'

Sylva could help and Flash, of course. She wasn't sure about Eddy.

'Sylva, go and get Walt. We need his help. Tell him it's to save Amber.'

'Help to do what?'

'We're going to build a mountain. At least, it's got to be a pile big enough for a human to notice. We've got to grab their attention.'

Flash looked unconvinced – they were rarely on the same thought wave. While Sylva was gone, Molly explained what she had in mind.

Eddy was touchingly confident in Flash's ability to build mountains. So, when Sylva returned, Flash went with her as assigned, to collect leaves and stems while Walter and Flo foraged in the other direction.

Molly pushed some gravel into a mound to start off their pile. When the others returned, she went with Walt to gather more branches.

On her return, it was disheartening to see how little their efforts had achieved. The bump was hardly noticeable to mirling eyes, yet Mother must see it with human eyes when she came to feed the fish in the morning. Dragging branches and leaves to the front of the tank had taken all their depleted energy.

Walter sounded apologetic. 'It won't be high enough.'

'No,' agreed Flash, looking pleased that someone else had said it first.

Walt and Flash added their branches to the pile, and Molly stood back to think again.

Flo stood by the glass wall with her hands clasped in front of her, gazing at the door of the living room where Andre stood, reluctant to drag himself from the TV and go to bed.

'Are you all right Flo?' Flash sounded concerned.

Flo shook her head as if to clear it. 'A silly idea. I thought I might be able to make Andre hear me, or at least sense something. I hoped if I c-concentrated really hard…'

Her eyes were red. 'I'd better go check on Grandad.'

Flash looked again at their mound, which had already settled flatter. 'We'll have to make it a platform instead. Or even a carpet.'

A bier, thought Molly. She tried to dismiss the image.

'Eddy, you see those three minnows skulking at the back, behind the stones?' He nodded. 'Do you think you could persuade them around to the front, to rest on our leaves?'

Eddy's smile curved at the prospect of being able to help. 'I can give it a go.'

But would it be enough to make a human look twice?

Slowly the mat of leaves and filaments spread, although it was still pitifully small.

A minnow drifted out from behind a stone with Eddy lying along its back, leaning to encourage it in the direction he wanted it to go. He slid off when its slender length was positioned over the leaves. Its tail overhung the green covering.

Molly stretched her aching back, hands on her hips, as Flash and Sylva arrived hauling a large flat leaf.

'That's brilliant! Put it in front of the minnow, so it's obvious. Eddy, the next fish will have to rest half on the gravel too, or the fish will hide the leaves.' She eyed the swaying mirling. 'Will you be able to manage another one?'

'No problem.'

If Flo were here, thought Molly, she'd never talk to me again.

Flo clearly thought it was safe to stay with Grandad since Eddy was too weak to do more than watch.

The third minnow followed the second as Eddy persuaded it out to the front of the tank where a patch of green surrounded the first minnow. Andre passed the tank, and the mirlings froze.

He glanced in.

Molly would never know if it was their greenery or the ailing minnows that caught Andre's attention, or else the fantail above them, who was having trouble swimming upright. Andre's brows drew together as if trying to remember what was different the last time he looked in.

'Dad, the p-pump isn't working. There aren't any b-bubbles in the aquarium.'

While he flicked the switch on and off at the wall, Molly took the opportunity to hustle the mirlings into cover.

Father came and repeated Andre's switch-flicking, before pulling a white block out of the wall. He went away and returned with a long metal tool, which he applied to the block.

'The fuse has blown,' he said. 'Must have been when the power came back after the cut.'

'Look at all the leaves under that minnow,' said Andre. 'Like a b-bed. Do you think the fish dragged them there?'

His mother had appeared in a long blue fluffy robe and was peering into the tank, 'I wouldn't know, son,' she said, 'but they'll need clearing out before they rot there. Those fish don't look too healthy either. If the pump's been off all that time, you should change some of their water.' She straightened up and added, 'I've just run my bath, so I'd better not leave it to get cold.' She left the kitchen, humming cheerfully.

Father grunted. 'Andre, can you get that plastic vacuum tube from the shed please – oh, and half fill the black bucket with water from the pond. Bring it in to warm up before it goes in the aquarium. I'll show you how to clean the gravel.'

'B-b-but Dad, I'm missing the film. I only came out to get a drink while the b-break was on.' His father's disapproving frown prompted a rebellion. 'I wish I'd kept quiet about the rotten old fish!'

His father grunted again and went to find the bucket.

16 Breaking Up

Andre was intrigued by the neat bed of plant debris that lined the gravel under the minnows.

To Flash's amusement, the boy had set up tests to discover how intelligent the fish were. He devised different barriers to the brine shrimps to see if the fish could get into them. He sat for ages, watching, which wasn't so amusing. The attention worried Molly and annoyed Flash, who couldn't swim when he wanted.

Eddy was itching to solve all the puzzles when Andre was in bed, but Molly forbade him to touch them. Molly's prohibition was enough to tempt Flash to move them all, but that would have led to even more human attention. Instead, he and Eddy annoyed Molly with suggestions about how they could confuse Andre, until Flo told them to stop sneering. Andre meant well.

Flash didn't want to upset Flo. She always listened to him and sometimes even asked his advice. Instead of worrying about everyone else, she should take more care of herself — although he wouldn't have minded if she worried about him occasionally.

Sometimes, when he swam down, he would see her gazing out through the glass, eyes fixed, brow creased in concentration, and he wondered what she was thinking about.

At supper one day, she asked them, 'If Andre did see us — properly, not when we're pretending to be fish — d-do you think he would help us? If we asked him.'

After a stunned silence, Flash asked, 'How?'

Flo's shoulders drooped. 'I don't know,' she admitted. 'I keep trying, but his mind doesn't hear me.'

Grandad was gentle. 'If they knew about us, they might want to keep us here and watch us.'

Sylva nodded. 'Like Beth with her fairground fish.'

That closed the discussion. Even Flash wasn't desperate enough to risk becoming an exhibit in someone's water zoo.

By the time the children broke up from school again, Andre had given up his experiments.

Flash's relief at this may have been the first time he agreed with Molly about anything.

They were equally relieved when the family didn't go away at half term. And, again, when the family spent the Easter holidays at home. Weeks passed without incident.

Flash had resumed his night-time breathing exercises. Each night he also added a little more to his new length of cord that he was planning to loop around one of those drawer handles to support him to the floor. The cord was becoming heavy. How much more would he need to reach the floor?

His escape bid would have to be at night, but he was sure he could get under the closed door. When the door had been open, he'd seen a brush-like strip on the bottom to keep out draughts. There must be a gap under the door, or there would be no draught. The bristles looked like dried grass, and he could easily push his way through grass.

At night, the others would be asleep, which would avoid awkward questions.

Much as he wished he could take Eddy with him, he doubted his friend could make it as far as the floor, and there would still be the run to Mojo's water bowl.

Eddy would be heartbroken at being left behind.

But Flo would be heartbroken if Eddy disappeared overnight, not knowing what had happened or where they were.

Through the summer term, the children had tests or exams and outside the tank, tempers rose with the temperatures.

And then they were breaking up for the summer holidays.

Tempers cooled, but not the temperatures. Flash listened in to the family's breakfast conversation.

'Whew, it's hot, Dad! Can we have money to go swimming?'

Father grunted. 'Naturally, the year we book to go abroad is the year Britain has a heatwave.'

'The newspaper says it was hotter here yesterday than on Costa Del Sol,' said Mother.

Father pushed his empty plate away. 'I could have saved our money!'

Mother picked up his plate. 'It's sure to rain while we're away,' she said. 'It always rains on Bank Holidays.'

The water in the fish tank was warm as well. Flash recalled the pond's cool pockets in the deeps and among the waterfall's bubbles. Even in the hottest weather the pond would cool at night, but no evening breeze rippled the tank's surface.

Warm water held less oxygen.

Fish became more active at higher temperatures as their metabolism sped up.

Racing around like children at Beth's birthday party, they ate more and left more mess behind them.

With the children home from school, Mother sometimes lost track of how long it was since she last cleaned the gravel.

The water was getting harder to breathe. If he was leaving, it would have to be soon while he was fit enough to make the distance.

When Father brought home a new fish that died on its second day, Flash heard Mother point out they already had too many fish for the size of the tank. Neither suggested they buy a bigger one.

The children rarely paused to look in now. The fish had become as familiar as the wallpaper.

The pump stopped working, and Molly thought, here we go again. But this time Mother spotted it straight away.

It took Father most of the day to get the pump working properly. Mother kept out of the way until he'd fixed it.

'What was wrong with it?'

'Hanged if I know. Maybe there was a blockage. It seems OK now.'

'The gravel's due for a clean-out but it's getting late now. I'll do it tomorrow.'

When tomorrow came, a fantail was floating on the surface.

It floated into the drifting plant, so Mother didn't see it when she came to feed the fish.

Flipper from the pond was struggling to keep himself upright, and the darting cloud of minnows seemed smaller.

Two of them were skulking under the bridge when Molly went to find Flo.

Flo seemed jittery, as she poured out her concerns.

'Eddy's restless but he's g-getting out of breath very quickly. Walt says Amber can't stand up without losing her balance, and Grandad isn't t-trying to stand. He doesn't want to worry me, but he l-looks exhausted. They haven't had time to get their strength back before the pump's dying again.'

At the back of the tank, tiny bubbles had again slowed to a sad trickle.

Sylva swam over.

'Can you come? Walter's in a state. Amber's gasping and he's convinced she's dying.' She turned and hurried back ahead of them.

'I don't know what they think w-we can do,' confided Flo as they followed.

'Don't worry,' replied Molly. 'Walt always thinks Amber's dying.'

But this time Walt wasn't exaggerating.

Fish fed on the decomposing fantail.

When the family went to bed, Flash swam up to dislodge it from the plant that held it.

For the rest of that night, Molly listened to him coughing as he tried to clear the foul water from his gills. By morning, the former dodger-fish was also floating on the surface.

'Mum, two of the fish are dead. The p-pump's stopped working again.'

'Can you fish them out, Andre? I'll come in a minute.'

'What should I do with them? I'm sure there used to be more minnows too.'

Mother came to see for herself.

'Henry! The pump's stopped again. Fish are dying.'

Father appeared, muttering something Molly couldn't hear.

Andre said, 'The other fantails don't look right either. How come that fish from the fairground's still swimming around?'

He didn't wait around in the kitchen for an answer.

Father sighed. 'I'll get my tools.'

Mother said, 'What if it packs up again while we're away?'

When Father returned with his toolbox she said, 'Why don't we put them all in the pond?'

Hope flipped in Molly's chest. Flash was listening nearby, and their eyes met.

Father grunted. 'All the money I've spent on this fish tank,' he muttered, as he unhooked the pump and pulled out the tubing.

He took it all to the table. Mother brought him a mug of coffee.

Bethany came through on her way to the garden 'My friend Keisha loves our fish tank. She asked her mummy if she can have one just like it.'

'Well she's welcome to this one if she wants it,' said Mother, but Beth had gone.

17 Broken Down

As the morning dragged on, Flash returned to his lookout post in the drifting plant. Molly swam up to join him.

'How's the repair going?'

He shrugged. 'Father's muttering a lot if that's any clue. The children are keeping out of his way.'

She was about to leave again when Father put down his screwdriver.

'It's no good. We need a new pump.'

Mother said, 'When you go to get it, can you pick up a bottle of milk at the corner shop?'

Father stared at the bits of pump on the table.

'Did you want another coffee?'

'Uh – no. Thanks. Where's Bethany?'

'She's in the garden with Mojo,' his wife said.

Father got up and Molly heard him call from the back door. 'Beth, can you come here a minute?'

On the table he showed her the wreckage that used to be the pump.

'Honey, this pump is broken, and the fish are going to die while we're away on holiday. The only way we can save them is by putting them in the pond.'

'Can't you buy a new pump?'

'There won't be time to… um… order it and fit it in the aquarium.'

'Oh.'

'The fish would so enjoy being back with their friends in the pond.'

Molly wanted to point out that both pond fish were dead but, however fiercely she thought it, no human showed signs of hearing her.

'They'd have all that space to swim in the pond.'

'OK.'

'And you'd be able to see them anytime in the garden.'

'OK.'

Mother said, 'We'll do it now then, shall we?'

'OK.'

Beth skipped back out to the garden.

'Before she changes her mind,' said Mother.

'Too late now if she does. I've decided!'

Flash turned to Molly, and she read in his eyes the same hope that was growing in her.

They swam down to share it with the others, but their news came too late for Amber.

Sylva's cries reached them first, followed by Walt telling her there was no point wailing because Amber couldn't hear her. His tone was mild, but she recoiled as if slapped.

Now that the worst had happened, Walter was calm and winter-cool.

Flo comforted Eddy, while Grandad led Walt away from Amber's lifeless body. Nobody thought Molly wanted comforting.

She kept telling herself they might be going home. After all this time, a chance to return to the pond.

She couldn't yet believe that Amber wasn't coming with them.

When Flash told them the fish were to be released into the pond, Walt broke down in silent tears. Sylva hurried to comfort him, and they drifted away to the side of the tank, followed by fish attracted to their trail of tears.

Molly's thoughts skittered around her head. 'Will they just pour the fish in?' *Please let them just pour the fish in.* 'Or will they net them first?'

Grandad shook his head. 'The tank's too heavy for them to carry. We'll have to stay close to the fish.'

Flash pointed to the kitchen table, where the small fishing net lay in wait next to plastic bags and a large bowl. At the same time, the lid of the tank lifted, and two hands descended to the bottom of the tank, holding open a plastic bag.

Water poured into the bag, carrying with it two fantails, Walt and Sylva.

Father said. 'That's two we won't need to chase around the tank.'

He stood the bag in the bowl on the table, folding its top over the rim to stop it collapsing.

Mother said, 'They'd be easier to catch without the plants in there.'

She pulled the waterweed from the tank and Flo tensed.

'We came in on a p-plant.' She wiped her eyes with the wrist that wasn't across Eddy's shoulders.

'They might not put it in the pond though,' Molly reasoned. 'The plants are too small for humans to see them in the pond.'

'She's right.' Grandad struggled to his feet. 'The plants'd be lost in the pond. If the family gives the tank away, they'll likely give away the plants with it.'

Now Mother was removing the bridge and the big stones. The stones might be returned to the waterfall…

But how long would they be out of water? Molly tried to focus her thoughts.

'We need to be ready when the net comes. Flash, if you swim up with Grandad, I'll help Flo with Eddy.'

Flash stiffened, but after a moment, he nodded.

Satisfied, Mother stood by the kitchen table.

'OK. Ready for more fish,' and the net appeared above the tank.

Fantails were easy to catch. Father had netted three in one swoop before the mirlings swam high enough to catch the net. But now Flash realised that Grandad, and probably Eddy, were too weak to hang on to the net once it left the water.

'Wait at the surface, ready to drop inside when the net's underneath you.'

The fantails left the tank with some minnows, while Flash and Molly were still towing their charges the length of the tank.

'What now? Which side?'

Molly's panic didn't give Flash the satisfaction he might have expected. Watching Goldie still circling, he shared his thinking.

'This fairground fish won't be so easy to catch. She's faster than the fantails so she'll be harder to trap and the net will have to move around. Stay where you are and be ready to drop into it.' Flo looked as if she couldn't move far anyway. 'As soon as it's underneath you, dive.'

He linked arms with Grandad and pulled him farther along the side of the tank, so they wouldn't bump into each other.

Goldie flicked her tail angrily as the net hovered overhead.

He could grab the net from the outside, but would he be able to hold on to Grandad with only one free arm? And would Grandad's frail arm support the weight of his body out of water, swinging through the air?

While he considered his options, the net plunged again.

This time Father had one fish to target. It was probably luck that he correctly judged Goldie's response and collected her in a single swoop. Molly's group were in the right place. Pushing out from the side, they were caught up when the net rose and gone before Flash and Grandad reached them.

Three minnows still hovered over the gravel.

Minnows prefer to swim together, so they were likely to be caught together. This would be Flash's last chance to escape the tank.

Mother looked in from above. Her voice echoed around the glass walls.

'Let's take out more water. They'll have less space to escape to.'

The jug was overhead.

'Dive, Grandad! Don't get washed into the jug. They won't empty that in the pond.'

He grabbed Grandad and hurtled to the gravel, where they skulked in a corner with the minnows as the water's surface came closer.

'Don't worry … about me, lad … you go for it. … I can look out … for myself.'

Grandad had hardly been able to pull himself upright this morning but, although gasping, he was regaining his colour.

'I've been in … tight spots … before.'

It was tempting to accept Grandad's suggestion. Individually their chances of catching the net might be better.

His certainly would.

The net was back, dragging across the gravel to drive the minnows into a corner. As it approached, Flash grabbed Grandad's hand and pulled them both into it.

The net closed in on the minnows, dredging up gravel which covered the mirlings as the net rose from the tank.

Out of water, the gravel weighed more heavily on them. Flash fought himself free. Beneath him, Flo looked up from the depths of the bowl as the fish jostled above her.

Grandad was still under the gravel.

Flash kept hold of the netting as Father shook the minnows out. Some gravel fell with them, and there was Grandad, struggling to free a foot tangled in the net.

'Don't tip out any more gravel,' said Mother. 'It'll weigh down the bag in the pond.'

Grandad waved him away.

'Go, lad. Jump!'

Mother said, 'Leave the net in the tank.'

Flash began to clamber up the netting towards Grandad.

Once under water back in the tank, it was easy to release Grandad's foot now there was no reason to hurry.

18 Returning

Molly's group had been lucky. The net was directly beneath them when she tightened her arm around Eddy.

'Swim.'

She didn't let go of him until she felt the net pull them out of the water. Then she'd looked around for Flo.

Flo wouldn't lose sight of her brother, however exhausted she was. Still, Molly was relieved to see her friend drooping against the netting. She couldn't bear to lose anyone else.

Father inverted the net over the bowl, and they dropped with the fish into the water below. Sylva hurried to Flo, broadcasting her relief at their arrival, but Walt only nodded. Molly went to him.

'I'm so sorry, Walt, about Amber.'

'Not your fault.'

But she felt responsible for these youngsters who had been trapped with them. Could she have done more? Flo had enough to do looking after Eddy and Grandad.

Looking up, Walt must have seen her distress. Without warning he hugged her, as if seeking consolation as much as offering it. 'You did your best to keep us all safe.'

Molly grimaced at the memory. 'I must have been a pain in the gills.'

'Sometimes.' Walt released her and put his hands on her shoulders instead. 'You always seemed so... together. While most of us were falling apart.'

'It was all a front.' She shook her head. 'What use was I? I could have spent more time with Amber. If she'd stayed on the gravel with us, she might have been stronger – less exhausted. Maybe, if I'd asked her to help me, made it seem like fun…'

His brows lifted. 'That doesn't sound like Amber. She'd prefer fish-chase.' He almost smiled. 'It doesn't sound much like Molly either, come to that.' He unexpectedly kissed her nose. 'You did what you could.'

Gravel dropped into the water nearby, and three minnows swam down. Molly looked up, to catch Sylva watching them with narrowed eyes. Like the cat.

Mother's voice came from above. 'Don't tip out any more gravel. It'll weigh down the bag in the pond.'

Molly followed Flo's gaze to the net above them, which was little more than a blur to her eyes. When the blur moved away Flo muffled a cry.

Eddy looked up from where he was resting on the bottom. 'Is that all the fish?'

Molly didn't answer, but their eyes met.

'They didn't make it then.' Eddy hung his head. 'Amber's gone, and now Flash and Grandad.'

Flo knelt to take his hand, but the bag moved, tumbling them all at the bottom. Someone fastened it at the top and carried them through the kitchen to the back door. Molly couldn't make out details outside the bag, but she recognised daylight when they reached it.

Real daylight. Not just the memory of it through a window.

The bag floated on the surface of the pond, drifting at the shallow end. Inquisitive fish came to nose it.

Mirlings swam up to investigate. As soon as they were recognised, the waving and cheering began.

Someone must have told Molly's family.

They appeared, swimming around the bag until they found her and then waving and grinning like idiots. Her brother swam somersaults until Flo's family arrived and things calmed a little. Eddy made an effort to smile and wave back so as not to worry his mother.

Sylva didn't leave Walt's side. Molly saw him with his hands against the plastic, shaking his head at his parents, smiling and crying at the same time.

It seemed ages before Father pulled the bag over to the side of the pond. Sylva reached for Walt's hand and was still grasping it as they swam to freedom.

Unlike the fish, the mirlings knew what to expect when the bag was unfastened and were first to leave it, desperate to avoid being trapped inside after the fish had left. It would have been too cruel, having come this far, to be pulled from the pond in a collapsed bag and die in a rubbish bin.

Word had travelled around the pond. The reunions were draining.

Sylva told everyone – several times – how 'triffic' it was to be back, until Walt put a hand on her shoulder.

'Give it a rest, Syl.'

And she answered, 'Sorry, Walt.'

Her parents were looking old. On the way home she learned she was an aunt.

Her brother's partner was waiting with their son to greet her. They'd moved in among the roots of the home plant and were helping with the spawn beds, now the fry had hatched,

Friends arrived to hear her story. The afternoon was turning into a pond-wide celebration. Someone told Molly that Amber's parents were looking for her, and she slipped away.

She swam to the shallows under raindrops stippling the pond's surface. The rain quickly grew heavier, churning the upper water as she swam. Thunder rumbled.

Her brother had clearly been proud of his family. She hadn't expected him to embrace domesticity so quickly. Perhaps she would feel like that about someone one day and follow his example. She told herself that if she did, it would be because she wanted to, not because it was expected of her. She wasn't sure she believed herself.

Had the tank changed her? She had yearned to be home, but now she was here she didn't want to settle back into the old life. She had no idea what she wanted instead.

She felt untethered, adrift.

Surely, after facing genuine dangers and real tragedy, she had escaped the pond's expectations and could stop worrying what people thought of her.

She should have taken more notice of Amber. She should have looked after her.

She didn't dare imagine what Sylva was saying about her.

19 Rain

Father had dropped the net in the empty tank where it slid down to lie flat on the gravel. The tank had tipped sideways, and the jug dipped to collect more water.

Once Flash had freed Grandad's foot, they scrambled to higher ground, staying well behind the jug while still under water.

Its level was dropping fast. From somewhere in the kitchen, Mother said, 'You won't get much more out with the jug. You could try the syphon.'

The tank levelled and lifted from its shelf.

'It's light enough to carry now,' said Father. 'Where do you want it?'

'Out in the garden where it won't be in the way. Keisha's mum said she might pick it up before we go.'

A thin layer of water slopped across the gravel as Father carried the tank to the garden. He left it by the shed where the ground was uneven, and water drained from the raised side to pool on the other.

He came back twice, bringing the vacuum tube and the plants, which he left with their roots in water.

Flash couldn't see Amber's body. She may have been buried by the gravel when the tank was tipped. They kept to the deeper water.

'We need to get out of here, lad, or we'll find ourselves in some other house with no hope of ever getting back to our pond.'

Flash had been wondering if he could somehow scale the smooth glass walls. 'Or else we'll be poured down a drain when they clean the tank.'

They both knew that was a likely scenario.

Rain began to fall, gently at first, cooling the warm layer of water in the tank. Flash breathed in the reviving oxygen. Grandad lay with his eyes unfocused above a blissful smile.

The sky lit up, and an angry crash of thunder followed, grumbling into the distance as rain fell in earnest. The sky lightened again, and this time the thunder came sooner, crashing overhead as rain drove into the tank. Slowly the water level rose.

Flash and Grandad bumped fists.

Flash pulled off two filaments of weed, offering one to Grandad, and they made themselves comfortable.

When the rain stopped the tank was half full. The clouds cleared quickly after the storm, but the sun had set by then, and a full moon lit the garden.

Grandad shared his thoughts. 'Is it likely to rain again before someone comes to collect this tank?'

'Is someone going to collect the tank before the family go on holiday?' Flash wondered. 'They didn't seem sure.'

'Good question.' Grandad nodded, looking around him. 'We're all right for food. Plants'll stay fresh. Now there's water in here, we can reach that fern on the driftwood too.'

Flash considered the angle of the tank.

'If the rain got to the top, maybe we could throw ourselves over.'

'I dunno. Seems a risky sort of strategy to rely on. It'd take a lot of rain and we might not get any more?'

Both reflected silently until Grandad posed another question.

'Assuming you gets your rain, what happens when we gets to the top?'

'It's a long drop,' Flash had to admit. 'We could walk that rim around the top and slide down the side that's leaning back a bit.'

The tank wasn't leaning much; could Grandad manage such a steep slide? The old mirling hadn't been daunted by the suggestion. Flash saw he was nodding to himself, so he raised another possibility.

'Do you think you could make it to the pond from here?'

'Hmm, maybe,' replied Grandad. 'Don't let me stop you trying.'

His sharp eyes held Flash's. 'You could've been back in the pond by now if you hadn't wasted time trying to get me outa that net.'

Flash shrugged. 'Flo wouldn't have forgiven me.' Praise had never embarrassed him before. 'Molly would have had me kicked out of the pond.'

'You're fond of Flo, aren't you?'

'I'm fond of you all. You're the nearest thing I've got to a family.'

He'd known Grandad longer than he'd known his family. 'You had a family in the river, didn't you? When I arrived in the pond it was freedom for me, but to you it must have been like captivity.'

'Not like the tank was. But yes, it was hard. I was angry for a long time. Still, there's no denying I'd be fish food before now if I'd stayed in the river.'

Flash was thinking about that when Grandad added, 'I don't think I'd have lived much longer in that tank either. I wouldn't have wanted to.'

Flash agreed. 'We depended on the humans for everything. Whether they fed us or cleaned the tank… whether they even remembered to look at us.'

'They meant well. They din't know enough.'

'They could learn.' Flash remembered Father's leaflets and manuals at the beginning. 'You can't just give up when people depend on you.'

'They din't know about us though, lad.'

'The fish were their responsibility, and they knew about them.'

'The pond depends on 'em too.' Grandad pointed out. 'Only things take longer to go wrong.'

Flash was wondering how far away the river was when Grandad broke into his thoughts.

'Humans can muck things up in the river too, lad. There were a load of fertiliser got tipped in one time. Upstream, it were. It were watered down by the time it reached us, but dead fish washed past for days after, and we was all ill. Some of the old mirfolk didn't make it.'

Flash gazed through the glass where safety called from such a short, impossible distance.

'I'd settle for the pond right now. Do you think the others made it?'

Grandad nodded. 'That boy took the bag with fish in out of the kitchen while they was emptying water from this tank. I reckons they'll be safe home by now. That's thanks to you and Molly, although she wouldn't agree with me.'

Neither did Flash. 'I don't know how you figure that. I haven't managed to get you home yet.' He gestured around the tank. 'It was Flo who nursed you and Eddy through that bad water. Amber wouldn't have lasted as long as she did without Flo.'

Grandad nodded again. 'That's true. Flo gets on with things – no fuss. She has some good ideas too, and some that are more… wishful thinking. Flo thinks them up and Molly makes them happen.'

'Never mind what anyone else wants.'

'Sylva, you mean?'

But he hadn't meant Sylva. Gazing into the moonlit garden, he tried to decide what he had meant, while his gaze fell on a darker bump lying out there on the grass.

'Is that the ball the dog plays with? The one that's split?'

The big net had retrieved it from the pond many times. The ball lay now between the tank and the pond. Flash pressed his face against the glass, trying to see more clearly.

He turned to Grandad. 'Do you think you could last long enough out of water to reach that ball?'

'I reckon I could.' Grandad nodded. 'What have you got in mind?'

'I think the split's at the top right now – see it's darker? There'll be rain in it. Maybe enough to take a breath and rest before the last dash to the pond.'

Grandad's eyes shone in the moonlight. 'I'm up for it, lad, if you can get us out of here.'

20 Getting It Wrong

Molly found Flo and Eddy sitting in Grandad's hollow, backs hunched and heads drooping.

The faces that rose to greet her wore identical expressions of misery. It was the first time Molly had noticed any family resemblance.

'You're looking better,' she told Eddy. 'How do you feel?'

'Alive?'

She changed the subject.

'How's Walt?'

Flo answered.

'He's relieved to be home, like the rest of us. Then he remembers Amber isn't and feels guilty. Sylva's looking after him.'

They sat against Grandad's reeds and savoured the fresh water, cooled by the storm. Daylight rippled between the dancing bubbles of the waterfall that she'd feared she would never see again.

Grandad had loved this spot.

Flo's red-rimmed eyes found Molly's. 'Where do you suppose Grandad and Flash are?' The question was desperate with hope. 'I saw Father put the net back in the tank.'

There was something different about Flo.

Molly told her, 'Flash is a survivor.'

'Yes,' Eddy roused, 'and he'll look after Grandad.'

Flash was more likely to look after Flash, but Molly didn't share that thought with the others. Flo must have read it, though, from her expression.

'Yes, he will look after Grandad. You didn't see, did you? When we were in the bowl on the table, Flash was in the net with the minnows. I thought he was going to jump.'

Eddy straightened, shocked. 'Why didn't he?'

'I don't know. Grandad was in the net too. When they took the net away, they were both still in it.'

Flo always tried to see the best in everyone. Perhaps she had misinterpreted what she saw. Eddy was nodding.

'He looked after us too. He was patient with Amber – with both of us when we were tired. He helped us build up our strength. When we needed to rest, he'd put on a show for us, clowning around the fish until we were ready to swim again. Without Flash, we wouldn't have lasted as long as we did.'

'It must've been hard to be patient when he was so wound up himself.' Flo wasn't stammering – that was the difference. 'He was like that toy car of Joel's that shoots off when he lets it go.'

'Only there was nowhere he could shoot off to.' Eddy nodded at Flo. 'If anyone can bring Grandad home, Flash can.'

Were they talking about the same Flash? When had he changed? How had she not seen?

It was too late to be sorry now.

Flash woke next morning to a glorious blue sky overhead. Grandad was up already and stood gazing through the glass. Flash joined him.

The pond looked so close.

'Looks like there's new plants since we left.' Grandad turned from the pond to meet his eyes. 'Once we're outa this tank, lad, it's every mir for hisself.' His hand rested briefly on Flash's shoulder. 'You've done enough.'

He turned back to take in their view of the garden. 'At least if I don't make it back to the pond, I've ended up under an open sky, not some flat, unchanging ceiling.'

For breakfast they broke a fresh shoot from a slow-growing water plant: the one they used to save for special occasions, or to tempt a sick mirling to eat. Over breakfast and through the morning they re-examined their options for getting out of the tank. A shower raised their hopes but ended quickly and the sun came out again. The clouds that passed across it now were the white, fluffy kind that promised no rain.

The door of the house opened, and Mojo bounded past. An unfamiliar voice drew nearer. Flash had to concentrate to recognise the words.

'…can't thank you enough. Keisha has been going on for weeks about Bethany's fish tank. My brother keeps tropical fish, and she spends ages watching them when we visit him.'

'You know what you're letting yourself in for then,' answered Father's voice. 'We can't offer you a pump, I'm afraid. It's packed up.'

'So Abby said. But I can afford a pump – maybe even a heater if I don't have to buy all this.'

'I'll carry it out to your car. Is it open?'

'I'll go and unlock it,' said Keisha's mother.

Flash turned to Grandad, but the old mirling was already on his feet.

'I'll just tip out the rainwater,' said Father, 'and I'll be right behind you.'

A chance.

Their last chance.

Father tipped the tank to lay flat and water gushed over its metal rim. Flash and Grandad made sure it carried them with it over the rim and across the grass.

The mirlings couldn't afford to waste oxygen hiding from Father, but as they ran through the grass, Father struggled to lift the tank and didn't notice them.

The grass had been mowed recently, so they could see the ball as they ran. Where the tank had emptied, wet grass kept them cool and moist for half the distance. Flash supported Grandad for the last few steps, pushing him over the edge of the split into the ball.

'Can I help?'

Keisha's mother was back, but Father said he was fine and lifted the tank from the garden table where he'd rested to get a better grip.

'It's a lovely waterfall,' she said, admiring the pond as he led the way. 'Will those fantails survive out here in the winter?'

'Maybe. If it doesn't freeze. You're welcome to them if you want them when your tank's set up. We can fish them out when we're back from Spain.'

'Thanks for the offer,' said Keisha's mother, 'but I'm thinking I might get a heater and go for livebearers – guppies or mollies.'

Their voices faded as Father staggered down the side of the house, followed by Keisha's mother.

Through the split, Flash watched them go. He dropped back into the ball and submerged himself to breathe. There wasn't much water in there, but it was enough to keep them alive while they rested.

They lay with their gills in the water, and Flash tried not to show his impatience while Grandad recovered. He hoped he hadn't got this wrong.

The pond looked farther away than he'd first thought.

He wasn't going without Grandad now, though, even if he had to carry the old mir to the water's edge.

Grandad nodded. 'Let's go for it.'

The split above them darkened.

Yellow eyes looked in.

21 Cats and Dogs

Flash had looked into those eyes before. Would the cat see his bright colours in the dark of the ball?

The eyes withdrew. Flash held his breath.

The ball rocked.

It rolled, tumbling them over each other. When it stopped, most of the water was gone and one end of the split was lower. If it tipped farther, they would lose all their remaining water.

'Grandad, you OK?'

'Yep. Is this thing moving in the wrong direction?'

'I think so.'

'So do I, lad. I think it's time we made a run for it.'

Flash thought so too, but he was no longer sure which direction the pond was. Could Grandad make it? Once out of the ball, they could lose precious seconds deciding which way to run.

And there was the cat.

The cat would notice Flash's orange before Grandad's bronze, which might give the old mirling a fighting chance. They didn't have much time to decide.

'If we rolls again, we can drop through the split.' Mojo's bark came from the direction of the house. 'Then if we stays still in the grass till cat's gone it might not spot us.'

Flash knew Grandad couldn't do that for long and still make the pond.

The barking headed towards them and past them.

The ball hadn't moved. Mojo had chased the cat away.

Relief washed through Flash, emptying his thoughts. He was climbing to look out when the split darkened again, and a long tooth speared through the gap. It brushed his side, forcing scales back and tearing his skin.

They rose from the ground.

The ball travelled at a jog. Sounds around them changed. Mother's voice rang out.

'Mojo's leaving a water trail. What've you got there, boy?' The split lightened as she took the ball from the dog's mouth. 'It's his old ball. Ugh, there's bugs in it. Outside, boy!'

They flew through the air, flung from one side to the other as the ball turned and the last of the water drained away.

'Hold on, Grandad!' (Hold on to what?) 'Try to hang on to the edge of the split.'

A bone-shaking jolt shook the ball as it hit something and bounced.

Molly revelled in the luxury of waking up in the pond, with fresh water to breathe, space to grow and nobody relying on her. It was over, she told herself. She was safe.

She forgot to be wary.

'Molly, we were sorry to miss you last night.'

His mother began. 'We wanted to thank you for looking after Amber. And Walter.'

She gave a sob, and her husband took over. 'He told us how you looked after them. We know you did your best.'

Molly was hot with embarrassment. 'It was Flo who looked after Amber when she was ill, and Eddy kept her safe when they went swimming.'

But Amber's mother wasn't to be side-tracked. 'Sylva told us how you'd mothered them – those were her words. And how you listened when she needed someone to talk to.'

Her husband continued. 'Walter is afraid you're blaming yourself.'

'He's blaming himself, poor soul.' His wife hiccupped. He put an arm across her shoulders and carried on.

'They've told us how you organised everyone to keep them safe.'

By the time Amber's parents left, Molly was almost as tearful as they were.

Until now, she had been in control. When she swam out of the plastic bag yesterday, she had allowed herself, for the first time, to believe the nightmare was over. She was safe.

But Amber wasn't.

The more she tried to forget about the tank, the more her thoughts kept returning to it. Every recollection of Amber, Grandad, even Flash, brought another pang of regret. She needed to get away from her family's constant questions.

Feeling increasingly remote from the continuing celebrations, she swam again to the shallows to watch the waterfall's bubbles plunge and resurface. Freedom felt unexpectedly empty.

Flo found her there, clasping the horn-shaped trophy Grandad had polished to a shine. It no longer shone. She had found it there along with the crown, which was rotting now. There was no sign of the blade.

'Are you all right, Molly? You look glum.'

'Oh Flo!' She shook her head. 'I'm so glad to be back I should be swimming somersaults.' She gulped. 'But Grandad should be here. It isn't fair.'

She clasped the trophy to her chest. 'And Flash. And Amber…'

'I wish we'd known Amber before.' The sweep of Flo's arm encompassed the shallows with the waterfall's end and the view towards the deeps. 'Here, in the pond.'

'How is Eddy?'

'Angry – with himself, mostly. He thinks he should have been with Flash, helping to bring Grandad home. He's gone to the pump this morning.'

'Is that wise?'

'I don't think he's strong enough yet, but…' Flo shrugged. 'Yesterday, one of his old tormentors referred to Amber as "that cripple" and Eddy punched him.'

Molly's eyes widened and Flo nodded. 'Exactly. He had the advantage of surprise, of course. The guy fell into the path of a streaking fish and ended up in the reeds.' She gave a mirthless laugh. 'The cretin's wife gave him a swipe when he picked himself out, which their daughter thought was funny.' She sighed. 'So he cuffed the tiddler for laughing.'

She looked around them. 'I came to sweep out Grandad's place.'

Molly followed her gaze.

'I suppose the plants will grow through again now.'

'I thought it might be good to keep the place cleared, as a sort of meeting place. A memorial to Grandad.'

Molly nodded. 'That's a nice idea. It was our meeting place, wasn't it – when he was… here.'

She looked down at the trophy she was cradling. 'Why don't we hold an annual tournament – like he wanted – and name it after him.'

Flo looked uncertain. 'The Grandad Games? What *was* his name?'

Molly shook her head. 'Maybe it's a daft idea… I just need to be doing something.' Which was odd, considering how much effort she used to put into doing nothing.

'I was thinking of setting up reed shooting sessions for youngsters.'

Flo frowned. 'Is that wise? What if some little bruiser decides to shoot gravel instead of water?'

'It would be too heavy to blow far. In the pond, the water would slow the pellets, and out of it, they can only hurt the idiots who stay up there to be shot at. It would give the lively ones something to do out of school, instead of preying on weaker youngsters.'

She lay the trophy reverently against the reeds. 'Tiddlers need to learn that it's okay not to be a winner. Everyone has different strengths. I've been talking to my brother too, about the kids that play kickabout on the pond floor. He and his mates used to have rules and everything. They're going to mark up a playing pitch and organise players into teams. Teams are good for learning to work together.'

Flo was impressed. 'You've really thought about this.'

She was still thinking. 'I want to get schools involved. It's time tiddlers learned about more than herding fry and what's safe to eat and how to bully their classmates.'

Eddy swam into view.

Flo sighed. 'He can't have lasted long at the pump.'

In the sky above Eddy, a blur passed over the pond. A bird, or maybe the shadow of a bird, hit the outer wall of the waterfall and rolled into it.

Eddy touched down and wandered over to them, kicking at pebbles and debris as he came. Molly thought he looked like Joel when he'd been told off.

'Hi, Eddy.'

A pebble dropped into the water behind him. They all looked up.

Down the waterfall, the blur was gathering speed, skipping every time it hit a stone. It bounced off the last boulder and sunk through the water. Molly could now see it was the wreckage of a ball, rising with the bubbles to float just under the surface.

As it bobbed in the wash from the waterfall, a vivid orange mirling with a black streak swam out of a slit in its side and zigzagged to the bottom of the pond where he sat looking dazed.

22 Riding the Current

With one thrust of his tail, Eddy was beside him. 'Flash…
how…? Magic! I should have known.'

Flo joined them. 'You're bleeding. Let me look at that.'

She looked up with concern in her eyes. Flash moved
his hand away and watched her kneel to inspect the wound
in his side.

Of course. Shows of strength and feats of heroism
would never be the way to get Flo's attention.

But now he put his hand over hers and rose to his feet.
She rose with him as he turned from side to side, staring
out into the water. 'Where's Grandad?'

She stepped back. 'Is Grandad with you?'

He launched like a reed-shot to the surface, where the
ball was bobbing away from the waterfall. Eddy followed
him inside it but by then Flash had seen it was empty. He
swam out as Molly and Flo reached them.

'Are you sure he didn't fall out over the pond?' He
turned again, searching. 'Maybe when the ball hit the
water?'

Molly squinted up at the waterlilies in case he'd landed
on one. 'I didn't see him. But I miss a lot.'

Flo eyes were skimming the surrounding waterscape.
'Neither did I.'

Think! 'He must have fallen out while we were in the
air.'

Flash followed Molly's eyes to the waterlilies. No, Grandad could have rolled into the pond if he'd landed on a lily pad.

New plants had changed the waterscape. Stems trailed into the pond from a patch of ground cover beside the waterfall.

'Maybe he's in the garden.'

Eddy called, 'Flash, what are you doing?'

He was already climbing but dunked his head under the surface to reply, 'I may be able to spot him from here.'

'And then what?' asked Molly. Her words hardly reached him through the air. 'You can't just… run out and get him.'

Eddy started to follow, shouting, 'There's nothing you can do, mate.' He slid back into the pond, too weak to climb far out of water.

Flash turned to check his friend was safe. Flo nodded to him as she joined Eddy and he returned to his search for footholds between pebbles slippery with blanketweed.

He climbed up the waterfall and around its curve, losing sight of the pair below.

Needing to breathe, he hooked one arm around a firmly lodged pebble and submerged his gills in the turbulent water.

As he came up again, he thought he saw eyes peeping around a stone.

How far up was the ball when it hit the waterfall? It had felt like a long roll down.

He could see no eyes up there now. Must have been his imagination.

Wishful thinking.

Clinging to the stone, he began a careful turn to search the garden, but his eye caught movement in the channel above and he twisted back.

His feet slipped and he clung to his stone with all the strength in his webbed fingers.

'Whoopee-ee-ee!'

The cry drew nearer.

Skeltering down the waterfall, veering between stones and slithering over blanketweed, Grandad's tail thrashed like a dodger's.

'Just like the riv-e-e-r...' Flash caught, as Grandad bounced past, swerving just in time around the stone at the end.

He heard a tiny splash among the tumblings of the water, before Eddy's 'Yay!' filled his head.

Flash threw himself into the waterfall and hurtled after Grandad.

If you have enjoyed *Pond People*, please leave a review on
Amazon.

About Cathy

Cathy Cade is a former librarian who began writing in retirement. She lives with her husband and dogs in Cambridgeshire's Fenland most of the time (with two garden ponds) and occasionally in a suburb of London, across the fence from Epping Forest.

Her acquaintance with fish began, like so many mothers, with a fairground goldfish, progressing through coldwater and tropical indoor tanks to the sludge and blanketweed of outdoor fishkeeping. She has yet to meet a mirling but keeps looking.

Cathy's writing has been published in *Scribble, Best of British, Tales of the Forest, SirensCall, Writers Forum, SevenDays, The Fens, Flash Fiction Magazine, The Poet* anthologies, and *To Hull and Back Short Story Anthology 2018*, as well as in collections from the Whittlesey Wordsmiths writers' group. Her books, *The Godmother, Witch Way, and other ambiguous stories* and *A Year Before Christmas* are available from Amazon and Smashwords.

Find Cathy online at www.cathy-cade.com

Other Books by Cathy…

See https://books2read.com/godmother

The Godmother

Euphemia Ffinch, godmother to Lucinda Eleanor, has been travelling since she retired as nanny to the Regalian royal family.

Buttons the dog lives in the basement with Cindy since his master died. Cindy's stepmother treats her as a servant and is no dog lover.

Prince Alfred of Regalia is dreading his birthday ball. His stutter gets worse in company, and the daughters of the nobility look down on him. They are all taller than he is. He'd rather invite the girl he met online.

Euphemia learns that Cindy's father has died. Her intuition tells her she is needed back in Regalia.

But Cindy hasn't read the fairy tales and has plans of her own. Somebody has other plans for Euphemia too, and Buttons isn't sure he has a future to plan for.

"A lovely short story with some humour and twists to the plot that makes it a pleasure to read." – Sally Cronin

Available from Amazon and Smashwords

Short stories with a question

Witch Way

and other ambiguous stories

Cathy Cade

A motley collection of characters who aren't all they seem
– or are they? You decide.

Meet mirlings and brownies, a citizen of Pompeii, an unsettled soul, a misguided confidante, an unlikely Samaritan, a trainee mortician,

and a witch... or not.

'An eclectic collection … varied and entertaining', *Sally Cronin*;
'Have reread it several times', *Goodreads*;
'…had me on the edge of my seat … Definitely worth a read';
'A little gem of a collection', *Amazon*;

Available from Amazon and Smashwords
See also https://books2read.com/witch-way

A Year
Before Christmas

by

Cathy Cade

Emmie the Elf works hard, running errands and sweeping out reindeer stalls, but Santa's newest helper still finds herself grounded on the biggest night of the year.
Can Emmie get airborne in time for next Christmas Eve?

'Would make a great stocking-stuffer gift,' John Spiers
.'A lovely story', Amazon review.

Available from Amazon and Smashwords
See also https://books2read.com/yearbeforechristmas

Riding the Waterfall

Bonus verse

Skimming down the waterfall, bouncing off the pebbles,
Sun has roused the pondlings for forbidden winter revels.
Hair streams like blanket weed; scales spark like ice.
Legs thrusting like a fishtail through the water slice.
From shallows' warmth to chill depths where the fish don't stir,
We pass between, attracted by the pond pump's whirr.

Bodies cooling, thoughts grow heavy, yet we watch and listen;
Fight the pump's drag till a gap shows
where the fan blade's missing.
Then up the snaking tunnel, poured into the filter box,
To skid across its slimy foam and dive beneath the floss,
Gills closed against the sludge, with pounding heart and brain,
Spewed out, to skitter down the waterfall again.

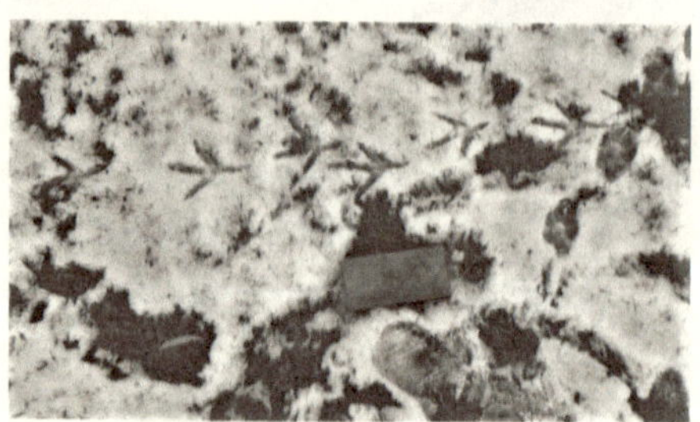

Children scamper from the house through freshly fallen snow.
'Dad, Big Bird's been here on our grass.
Look! Footprints in a row.'
Father comes to view the tracks – a spur and three sharp toes.

Pond People

'Looks like a Heron after fish. He stood here by the pond
To watch but couldn't catch one through the reeds,
and now he's gone.
And you'll be late for school. It's time for breakfast now
– come on.'

All's quiet in the garden. One more turn before we're done.
Before the cold reclaims my soul, we'll chance another run.
The sun's moved round and left the pond.
Dark clouds are gathering too.
Those whirling blades seem faster now; we barely make it through
To ride the dark hose, surf the surge and join the water's fall.
But something's watching,
perched up on the channel's stone-clad wall.

Black beady eyes, a beak descending. Quick – between the stones,
Dodging and weaving as it strikes…

Under rocks, through channels… still we flee this dinosaur
Until – like music calling us – we hear the cascade's roar
And drop through churning water with no energy to jump,
Ready to sleep till Spring.
With luck, they won't have fixed the pump.

If you enjoyed this story please leave a review
on Amazon or Goodreads

From the Whittlesey Wordsmiths

Stories and verse from our writing group.
Available from Amazon